B

HERE
THERE BE
GHOSTS

Other books by Jane Yolen and David Wilgus

Here There Be Dragons
Here There Be Unicorns
Here There Be Witches
Here There Be Angels

Jane Yolen

HERE THERE BE GHOSTS

Illustrated by DAVID WILGUS

HARCOURT BRACE & COMPANY
San Diego   New York   London

B

Requests for permission to make copies of any part of the work should be mailed to: Permissions Department, Harcourt Brace & Company, 6277 Sea Harbor Drive, Orlando, Florida 32887-6777.

"It Was the Hour" and "Ghost Boy" copyright © 1998 by Jane Yolen; first publication. "Tombmates" copyright © 1989 by Jane Yolen; originally published in *Best Witches* (Putnam). "Police Report" and "The White Lady" copyright © 1998 by Jane Yolen; first publication. "The Boy Who Sang for Death" copyright © 1979 by Jane Yolen; originally published in *Dream Weaver* (William Collins Publishers, Inc.). "Seance for Eight" copyright © 1998 by Jane Yolen; first publication. "Mrs. Ambroseworthy" copyright © 1994 by Jane Yolen; originally published in *Bruce Coville's Book of Ghosts* (Apple/Scholastic), edited by Bruce Coville. "Night Wolves" copyright © 1995 by Jane Yolen; originally published in *The Haunted House* (HarperCollins), edited by Jane Yolen and Martin H. Greenberg. "The Singer of Seeds" copyright © 1989 by Jane Yolen; originally published in *The Faery Flag* (Orchard Books). "In the Silvered Night," "Mandy," "Haunt," "Green Ghosts," and "Souls" copyright © 1998 by Jane Yolen; first publication. "The Moon Ribbon" copyright © 1976 by Jane Yolen; originally published in *The Moon Ribbon and Other Tales* (Thomas Y. Crowell). "Prom Ghost" and "My Own Ghosts" copyright © 1998 by Jane Yolen; first publication. All reprinted by permission of the author's agent, Curtis Brown, Ltd.

Library of Congress Cataloging-in-Publication Data
Yolen, Jane.
Here there be ghosts/Jane Yolen; illustrated by David Wilgus.
p. cm.
Summary: An illustrated collection of short stories and poems about ghosts.
ISBN 0-15-201566-3
1. Ghost stories, American.   2. Children's stories, American.   3. Ghosts—Juvenile poetry.   4. Children's poetry, American.   [1. Ghosts—Fiction.   2. Short stories.   3. Ghosts—Poetry.   4. American poetry.]   I. Wilgus, David, ill.   II. Title.
PZ7.Y78Hj   1998
[Fic]—dc21   98-13732

Designed by Camilla Filancia and Linda Lockowitz

First edition   F E D C B A

Printed in the United States of America

To Lexi Callan, my foster granddaughter

Sometimes the best way
to exorcise one's ghosts
is to greet life with love and joy
as you surely do

Contents

HERE
THERE BE
GHOSTS

This poem had two starting places: the Bible's Book of Job and T. S. Eliot's great poem The Waste Land, *which I studied in college. But really I was trying to capture the disquieting experience of seeing a ghost. This was complicated by the fact that (1) I had never seen any such thing, and (2) it was morning—not the usual time for such visitations.*

It Was the Hour

It was the hour when night visions breed disquiet....
            —Book of Job, Ronald Knox translation

It was the hour of twelve,
ringing its steady way into night
from some undistinguished steeple
in the dark town behind us.
We walked a hand's breadth apart,
deep in conversation
about the nature of God.
Suddenly a brown-mantled,
hooded third, a shadow's shadow,
moon-called, bell-bidden,
stood between us.
"Who are you?" I asked.
But no voice informed.
Just the dark, the shade,
the disquiet, the fear,
the hairs on my arms
standing at attention,
as if answer had come indeed,

unmistakable in its single syllable.
        Ghost.
So near the word *guest,*
yet uninvited to our converse,
we shook with the raw intrusion.
Then the moon was put out by a cloud
as simply as a candle is snuffed.
Midnight's last change rung,
the visitor obliquely departed
leaving the space between us unfilled.
And we, without will or words to finish,
ran home, as dogs whipped without mercy
go to the comfort of light, of hearth,
and the perceived safety
of the good master's home.

There are three identifiable bits from real life in this story. First, I met a woman who told me she had heard angels on the street during some sort of seizure but had been given medicine that stopped her visions. She was glad. "Actually, the angels were quite terrifying," she said. Second, I have long kept an article in my Ideas file about the Collier brothers, recluses who lived for years in a house where they made paths out of stacked newspapers. Third, my father-in-law had had shock treatments for depression back in the 1950s. These three "story seeds" haunted me for years, finally coming together in this tale. Writers turn their ghosts into stories.

Ghost Boy

When my mom's younger sister, Aunt Louisa, was twenty-seven, she heard a choir of angels. She was on Madison Avenue at the time, crossing the street. It was so awful—in the old sense of the word— that she fell down right in front of a taxi and bit her tongue nearly in two. The doctor said it was a seizure and gave her a lifetime supply of medicine. She never saw or heard another heavenly concert again.

She stopped having dreams, too.

I remember her saying to Mom: "I don't miss the singing at all. It was the scariest thing imaginable. But I sure do miss my dreams."

Mom must have told me that story a hundred times. That and how Grandma Mildred used to see Emperor Napoleon, in his three-cornered hat, taking a bath in her tub on a regular basis. Saw him, that is, until she had shock treatments.

I don't want to have to take medicine that does away with my dreams. Or to be strapped down on a table and have my brains fried

3

with electricity. So I didn't tell Mom about the ghost Martin and I saw at the McConnell place last Tuesday.

I wasn't sure it was a ghost anyway. Martin said since we could see right through it, that proved it was a ghost. I told him you can see right through a window, too, which doesn't exactly prove a window is of the spirit world. So we agreed to disagree. But I still wasn't about to tell my mom. Radical treatments loom rather too large in our family's medical history for me to confess to something that odd without real proof.

But when we saw the ghost a second time, it seemed that confession was the better part of valor. So I told.

"Mom," I said, "what would you think if I told you I saw a ghost?"

Mom said, "I must call Lou about her doctor."

And I said, "Just kidding, Mom. April Fools." Though we both knew it was November.

Since my dad—who doesn't live with us but with a wispy blonde named Kimberleigh, who has protruding teeth and a nail-on-slate giggle—is a terrible practical joker, Mom really believed I was only fooling around. Or at least she said she did. She had had a lot of practice saying that during the fifteen years she was married to Dad.

But of course, I wasn't. Kidding, that is. Martin and I had seen *something.* Or had seen *through* something. Which is not the same thing.

And it just might have been a ghost.

The problem was that Martin and I had been where we weren't supposed to be. The old McConnell place is an abandoned mansion that is off-limits to the kids in town. It used to be home to the infamous McConnell brothers, two old recluses who collected newspapers and stacked them floor-to-ceiling everywhere in the house till there was only a narrow pathway from room to room. When the brothers stopped taking in the newspapers from their front porch

and it had been ten days since they'd last ordered in food from Ben's Big Groceries, a policeman went to check up on them. He found the two McConnells dead. One was big-time dead—that is, he had died months and months before and was only hair and bones. The other was recently dead. Ten days dead, to be exact, according to the coroner.

The brothers were buried together in Wildwood Cemetery, and then a long-forgotten niece came and threw out all the newspapers in the house. In the process, she found a fortune under the brothers' beds.

No buyer was ever found for the old place. Not in the eighteen years since the McConnells had died, anyway. The house had already been well into decay when they were alive; the gardens, never taken care of much before, had gone completely wild. The place was known locally as the Haunted House. Or the Ghost House. Or *That* House. There were signs all over the property about any trespassers being violated. But no one I knew was crazy enough to try to trespass. The McConnell house was just plain spooky.

Martin and I had done the McConnell brothers and their house for a Foxfire project when our class studied local history, so we knew a lot about it. I did most of the research and Martin did the writing. Our presentation was like a TV show, with me as the anchorperson and Martin the cameraman, using his dad's Minicam.

The day we got an A on our project—a first for both of us— we celebrated by riding our bikes to the McConnell house, and that's when Martin dared me to go in through a broken window we found around back.

Actually, he said, "So now we know it's just an old house, not a haunted house."

And I said, "Right. Old and ugly."

And he said, "Old and ugly and smelly."

And I said, "Old and ugly and smelly and spooky."

And he said, "Spooky? Well, I dare you to go in."

"You're kidding," I said.

"No I'm not," he said.

And he wasn't. After all, I *know* kidding. So of course I went in. I had to.

Not to be outdone by a girl, Martin came in right behind me.

It was after we had climbed to the second floor, avoiding the rotten steps in the staircase and fighting off a zillion spiderwebs, that we went into the back bedroom and saw the ghost.

It was *not* a ghost of an old man. Not a McConnell brother. We knew what they looked like from an old newspaper photo: shoulder-length grey hair and scraggly beards and broken teeth. It was a ghost boy, no older than Martin or me, with an odd bowl haircut, a white collared shirt, and flat, round glasses. And he was crying. Or trying hard *not* to cry. Which, if you are a thirteen-year-old boy, amounts to the same thing.

At first I thought that Martin had arranged a joke with a friend, though the boy was not anyone I recognized from school. Still, Martin comes from a big family. Lots of cousins. It could have been one of them. After all, the whole thing could have been a setup. Martin *had* dared me. And I sure knew *all* about elaborate practical jokes.

But when I realized I could see the wallpaper through the boy—a yellow wallpaper with sprays of daisies—I felt something funny in the pit of my stomach, which is not how I feel about practical jokes. I didn't say anything until Martin did, though. He would have made a comment about girls being wimps otherwise.

"Tess, it's a ghost," Martin whispered behind me. How he had suddenly gotten behind me I don't know, since he'd been leading the way till then.

"Don't be stupid," I said, thinking suddenly of my Aunt Louisa's angels and Napoleon in the tub with only his three-cornered hat on.

"You can see right through it," Martin said.

"Him," I amended.

"So . . ."

"You can see through a window, too," I whispered. But even I wasn't convinced by my argument. Only later, when rational thinking returned, I knew it had been a pretty cool answer.

And then the ghost turned his head and, with tears flooding from his eyes, opened his mouth and screamed.

Martin and I got out of there as fast as we could, tripping over the rotten stairs, bursting out of the front door, running through briars that clung stubbornly to our jeans. The briars turned out to be the only actual proof that we'd been anywhere off the main road.

We leaped onto our bikes and pedaled away even before our rears hit the seats.

Scared? We were *beyond* scared.

On the way home we only mentioned the ghost once, when we stopped to catch our breaths about a half a mile away.

Martin said, "What do you think it was?"

And I said, "I don't even *like* monster movies."

"You're a girl," he answered.

So I got off my bike and hit him. I had to. He knew it as well as I did.

We rode the rest of the way in silence, except for Martin's sniffles as he tried to suck up the blood that was dripping from his nose.

Martin called me later that evening. He rarely holds a grudge. Especially since I hadn't broken his nose this time. His voice sounded funny, though, because he wasn't breathing quite right yet.

"Tess," he said. "Did you tell?"

"No," I said. "Because of Aunt Louisa."

Martin is the only one who knows about her, outside of the family.

"Did *you* tell?" I asked in return.

"I said I ran into a tree. My mom looked at me funny."

"Maybe she doesn't believe about the tree."

"My mom always believes me," he said.

"Well, she won't if we tell her about the ghost. And besides," I said, "I'm not so sure we saw *anything*."

"But Tess..." Martin said. "We saw...we heard..."

"We have to go back to make sure."

He wasn't happy about it. I could tell because he was quiet for almost a whole minute. But at last he agreed, snuffling just a little.

And so we went a second time, the next day. We saw the see-through boy again. He was crying a little bit more. And when he saw us, he screamed a little bit louder this time. But not as loud as we screamed back.

We got out of there fast again—even faster than the first time—and hopped on our bikes. A few hundred yards down the road, I stopped. Martin stopped, too.

"Clearly a ghost," Martin said.

"Either that or a very good practical joke," I said.

"You can't see through those," Martin said.

He had a point.

We rode the rest of the way in silence; we didn't even say good-bye at the hedge that separated our two yards. I wasn't going to mention a thing, but then I asked Mom about ghosts. And told her quickly I was just kidding.

I picked up the phone and called Martin. "Tomorrow," I said. "And no screaming."

He knew what I meant, and he didn't contradict me. Part of me sort of hoped he would.

Which is how we got stuck going back a third time.

The third time was on Sunday, which I hoped would somehow have a mollifying effect on the ghost, it being the Sabbath. Not that either Martin or I are particularly religious. His family goes to church sometimes, but not as a regular thing. I only go when I am spending the weekend with my Dad and Kimberleigh and can't get out of it. Trust me—you do not want to listen to Kimberleigh singing hymns!

We brought along my mom's Bible; it's this pocket-size book, bound up in white leather, which she got from her grandmother for confirmation. We also brought along some of the xeroxes of newspaper clippings about the McConnell brothers, in case the ghost could read. And on the way, we stopped at Our Lady of the Elms Catholic Church and managed to get some holy water into Martin's Boy Scout canteen, though I told him it probably wouldn't work, him being a Unitarian and me a Methodist.

"Couldn't hurt," he said. Which made sense.

Without actually agreeing to it, we biked much more slowly than we ordinarily do, but we ended up at the McConnell house anyway. No matter what Einstein said about relativity, you still get there in the end.

The house squatted in its wild yard in an odd, glowering way. Or maybe we were just looking at it differently. The house seemed *really* spooky this time. That see-through boy had changed things. For good.

We left our bikes at the front door and dragged up the porch stairs, and every single step creaked. It was worse than a monster movie sound track. Then we went around back, and darned if every board in the porch didn't creak, too.

"Did it make this much noise before?" I whispered to Martin.

He shook his head.

"Or did we just not notice?" I asked.

He shrugged.

When we got to the broken window, he gestured for me to go in first, and I gestured back. Finally we tossed a coin.

I went in first.

To tell you the truth, it wasn't darker than before. It just *felt* darker. And it felt colder and damper and weirder, too. And I felt smaller and younger and weaker and...

Martin took my hand, which in other circumstances might have changed our friendship forever but now just felt steadying, though his palm was wet.

Wetter even than mine.

We went up the stairs side by side. And every step in that stairway creaked, too.

"I am *never* going to a scary movie again," I whispered to Martin.

He gave me this awful look, as if to say shut up, but he didn't open his mouth.

When we reached the bedroom door, we tossed the coin again. Only this time it fell on the floor and rolled away down the stairs, making more noise than you would believe.

So we walked into the bedroom together.

The ghost boy was sitting on the bed, staring out the window. He obviously hadn't heard the stairs creaking, me whispering, or the coin rattling down the stairs. Or else he didn't care.

Martin opened his canteen and shook holy water all over the ghost. But his hand was shaking so much, he shook the canteen loose, too, and it landed on the bed.

The drops of holy water never touched the ghost boy but fell right through him. However, the canteen bouncing onto the bed got his attention.

He turned around and opened his mouth to scream.

I said quickly, "Don't scream. You can't be any more scared than we are."

So he didn't. But he didn't close his mouth either. I could see that his teeth were small and even and not very white. Probably ghosts don't brush. Or floss either.

I said, "My name is Tess Harker, and this is Martin Carthy. Who are you?" It was not for nothing that I'd been the one who was the anchorperson in our Foxfire presentation.

The ghost boy closed his mouth and began to weep silently. I'd never known a boy to cry that much. But then I'd never known a ghost boy before. Maybe they're different.

I turned to Martin, who shrugged and dug out the xeroxes from his pocket. I took them from him and held them out to the boy.

"These clippings are about what happened in this house," I said. "And you aren't mentioned. So who *are* you?"

The ghost boy reached out to take the clippings, and they fell through his hand onto the bed.

So I did the only reasonable thing. I sat on the bed next to him, smoothed out the clippings so he could read them, and waited. But I slipped the Bible out of my pocket and set it between us, just in case.

Martin stood watching us silently. Well, not entirely silently. I could hear his raspy breathing.

When the ghost boy had finished reading the clippings, he looked up at me with these big dark eyes. There were no longer tears in them.

"I am Joshua McConnell," he mouthed, his voice as insubstantial as air. And then, as if his words had triggered something, he faded

even more, like a bit of daylight going into dusk. One moment he was there, and the next moment he was completely gone. There wasn't even an indentation on the bed to show where he had been sitting.

"*Joshua* McConnell?" Martin asked. "Who's that? The McConnell brothers were named David and Elijah."

"*I* know that," I said, shaking my head. "Remember—*I* did most of the research."

"So what do we do now?" Martin asked. He had on his I-give-up look.

"More research," I answered.

"We've already got our A," said Martin sullenly, gathering up the clippings from the bed. Now that the ghost boy had disappeared, Martin had no trouble speaking or moving.

"We got an A on a paper, not in ghost busting," I said.

"There's no ghost to bust," Martin pointed out. "He's already gone."

"Maybe," I said. "Or maybe not. But don't you just love a mystery?"

He smiled ruefully. "Better than a ghost story."

So we biked down to the library, but we couldn't find a mention of a Joshua McConnell anywhere. I already knew that. I am good at what I do.

"So now what?" Martin asked.

I snapped my fingers. "Hall of Records," I said.

"What's that?"

"Births," I said. "And deaths."

But it being Sunday, the Hall of Records was closed. Of course. So we went back to Martin's house and watched TV, though neither of us would look at anything scary. We'd done *enough* scary for one day!

However, after school the next day, we headed right to the Hall of Records, which is a big, old, yellow brick building next to the First Methodist Church.

And there we found out who Joshua McConnell was. A third McConnell brother, who had been much younger than the other two. And who had never died. At least there was no record of his death in the county, though his mother had died in childbirth.

"So he died somewhere else," Martin said.

"He *died* right in that house," I insisted. "And the brothers never told anyone he was dead. So there's no record of it."

Martin looked at me as if I was crazy. "Why didn't they mention it?"

"That's the big question number one," I said.

"And when they died, why didn't anyone mention it then?"

"Because by the time the McConnells died, they were so old and crazy there was no one around who remembered their little brother." Even when I said it, it sounded weak to me.

"Tess—it doesn't make sense."

"Then let's ask him."

"Who?"

"Joshua."

He shook his head. "You may be on a first-name basis with a ghost, but I'm not."

It took me almost an hour to argue Martin into going again. I had to promise to give him my Boiled in Lead T-shirt and my answers to the next true/false take-home exam in social studies. Plus I had to promise not to sock him in the nose again.

Martin's a hard bargainer.

15

This time up the stairs of the McConnell house, we didn't mind the squeaks. After all, we knew that nothing was going to get us there. We knew where the ghost hung out. And it wasn't on the stairs.

But when we got to the bedroom, Martin stayed in the doorway. I, on the other hand, went inside.

The ghost boy was not on the bed.

"Joshua," I called. "Joshua McConnell?"

And like mist over a mountain lake, he seemed to rise in vapor from the tattered and dusty bedcover, staring at me as he formed.

"You really need a different hairdo," I said.

He put an insubstantial hand up to his bowl cut but did not otherwise move.

I decided to get right down to the point of our return. "We couldn't find a death certificate for you," I said. "Though we found out when you were born."

The ghost nodded and I could see wallpaper daisies through his nose and chin. "I am mad," he whispered, starting to fade out even as tears began to run down his misty cheeks.

"Wait!" I cried. But if he heard me, he did not show it; and in a moment, he was gone.

"Don't you get it?" Martin said to me. "He's like your aunt."

"Which aunt?"

"You know—the one who saw the angels on Broadway."

"She only *heard* them. And it was Madison Avenue."

"Whatever." He made a face at me.

"Oh—I see. He thinks he's alive and we are some sort of . . ."

"Hallucination," Martin finished for me. "And clearly he has seen such things before."

"Wow!" I sat down heavily on the bed and coughed when the dust got up into my mouth. "So it was either keep him here at home or send him to . . ."

"The loony bin," Martin said.

We were both quiet for a long moment.

"Do you think," I said at last, "that they had shock treatments back then?"

"Or worse," Martin said.

I couldn't imagine anything worse. "Poor kid."

"So how can we help him?"

I goggled at Martin. "Help him?"

"Get rid of him. Exercise him." He made a motion with his arms as if he were chinning himself on bars.

"That's ex-*or*-cise, you dope," I said. "And I don't know how. The holy water didn't work. And . . ."

Martin looked at me sternly. "That's because we stole it from the church. We need a priest."

"I don't know any."

"Or a ghost buster."

"Ditto."

We stared at one another for a long time. Then Martin suddenly grinned.

"*Research*, Tess. You're good at that. We need books on ex-*or*-cism."

Which is how we spent the next week—even though it was spring break—in the town library.

Exorcism, we discovered, is the casting out of nonphysical entities. And while the person who performs the exorcism is usually a priest or a shaman or a magician, anyone can do it in a pinch, as long as they are careful and know the right way to go about it. The problem is that you can make things worse a lot easier than you can make things better. Of course, that warning seemed to apply to times when it is a demon one is exorcising, not a scared and unhappy ghost boy who had probably died fifty years earlier.

Armed with our new knowledge, Martin and I returned to the McConnell place and climbed the stairs with a kind of bouncy confidence.

We went into the bedroom and were a bit put out when the ghost boy did not materialize at once. We were in the middle of an argument about why he wasn't there, mostly consisting of my saying "Is!" and Martin saying "Is not!"—the kind of thing we used to do when we were five years old and fighting over lollipops—when the entire room seemed to take on a glow. It was an eerie glow, that sort of phosphorescent green you see in underwater movies.

And then a voice said sternly, *"Ille te expellit, cujus virtuti universa subjecta sunt."* It was not the ghost boy's voice.

"Who's that?" Martin asked as the voice droned on.

At the same time, I shouted, "Martin! Don't you know what that is?"

He looked at me, eyes wide.

"Someone is exorcising *us!*" I shouted. "Let's get out of—"

But it was too late. With a loud *whoosh*ing and a battering of heavy winds, we were taken up and tossed back in time, landing with a rather loud and jarring *thwack* on the floor of Joshua Mc-Connell's bedroom some fifty years in the past. At any rate, I thought it was that long ago. The bedroom was light and airy, the daisy wallpaper brand-new, and the bedstead well polished.

A priest in a long black gown was standing by the bed, a flask of water in one hand, a Bible in the other. When he saw us, he began muttering in Latin. At least I think that's what it was. We hadn't gotten much beyond *"Puella est bella"* in our Latin class.

"Begone, spirits," he said suddenly in English.

"We would if we could," Martin whispered back, which I thought was incredibly brave under the circumstances. I couldn't utter a word myself. But the priest did not seem to hear Martin over his own mumblings.

"Those are the very ones, Father," came a voice from behind us. I turned, and there was Joshua McConnell, standing in the doorway. "You see them, too, don't you?"

"I see them, Joshua."

"Then . . ." Joshua said with great relief and joy in his voice, "then I am *not* crazy."

"Not crazy, my son, but definitely possessed."

"Wait a minute!" I cried suddenly, anger overcoming fear. "*We* are the ones who are trying to exorcise *you!*"

At which both the priest and Joshua began muttering prayers like crazy, crossing themselves, and making a general mess of things. So I looked at my notebook and said the words I had jotted down to perform an exorcism.

"Spirits," I cried, lifting my right hand and sketching the sign of a cross in the air, "and things of darkness, by the power of Jehovah and all his angels, begone!"

And with a brief *pop!* they were.

I looked around. We were still in Joshua's bedroom, but the familiar tattered and cobwebby one, with the faded daisy wallpaper and the musty smell.

And we were alone.

Martin and me.

Definitely alone.

"Well . . . ?" I asked.

19

"Well..." he answered.

We turned as one and ran down the stairs.

We never went back to the McConnell place. We didn't have to. I checked the records again at the town hall, and the newspapers. And I found something I had missed before. Joshua McConnell had not died in that house. He had become a priest. Father Joshua had flown in from Detroit to officiate at his brothers' funeral. For all we knew, he was still alive and doing priest-type work in the Midwest: baptizing babies, giving sermons...even exorcising demons.

After all, he had learned to do that sort of thing successfully when he was quite young.

About twelve years ago I wrote a book of Halloween poems called Best Witches *that included the following poem. I began with the punny title, and the whole thing seemed to write itself from there. Is this a poem about real life? I have had a number of roommates—during college; after college; and since 1962, my husband, David. We have all been equally the clutter kind. I have never roomed with anyone I might charitably call "a tidy sort."*

Tombmates

I am a tidy sort of ghost,
But *she* likes clutter, muss, and mess.
I wear a clean and ironed shirt.
She wears a rags-and-tatters dress.
I never leave my chains around
But hang them up when not in use.
She leaves hers lying anywhere,
And heaps upon me such abuse.
She calls me "White Eyes," "Booger Ben,"
She calls me "Mausoleum Breath."
I tell you, she has really made
It hard to come to terms with death.
Do you think that there might be
A single in Eternity?

When I was a teenager in Westport, Connecticut, my friends and I used to sit and picnic on a long, flat, black marble tombstone belonging to someone named Agnes. We didn't need to climb over the wall into Willowbrook Cemetery, however, as the gates were always open and the groundskeeper did not have a dog. I used the picnic idea years later in a picture book called Letting Swift River Go, *but that was for an historical book, not a ghost story.*

My parents are buried in Willowbrook Cemetery, side by side, so I visit them, not Agnes. In fact, I do not even remember exactly where the Agnes stone is. Either my memory has misplaced it, or the stone has—spookily—misplaced itself.

Police Report

I'll try to tell it the way it happened, sir, but you know what a funny thing memory is. I mean, you must work all the time with witnesses who contradict one another. Exaggerations aren't new to you.

But what is true is that my best friends, Billy and Maddison, and me went to Willowbrook Cemetery last night. And we saw something flitting around the tombstones. Something white and wispy and insubstantial, I think the word is. Though whether it was a ghost, I can't really say, since ghosts aren't real. And what we saw *was*. Very real.

So call it what you want.

Why Willowbrook? Well, it's close to all our houses, and it's free. Pretty good recommendations, if you ask me.

We go to Willowbrook to sit on the old Agnes Doubleday grave because it's a slab of black marble that has soaked up sun all day long. When there's sun, that is. So it's real warm, almost like a little heater, all the way into early winter.

And that's where Billy and Maddison and me tell one another what happened during the day.

Yes, I suppose we could do that on the phone. But Madd's got three nosy little sisters and Billy's mom does computer stuff at night and needs the phone free for her modem. And my dad only lets us kids have three minutes each on the phone after seven, unless it's homework. He's real tough that way.

So Madd and Billy and me meet at the graveyard, which is right around the corner from all our houses, at seven every night—until it gets too dark and cold. We've been doing it for three months now: August, September, October. And yes, I know, last night was Halloween.

This is not a joke, sir. I wouldn't call it malicious mischief, no. I am simply telling you what I saw. Not kids in white sheets. Not a high school prank. Not three ninth graders scared of their own shadows.

I arrived at Willowbrook first. We're too old for trick and treating and costumes, and none of us wanted to go to the high school dance. But as it was Halloween, Billy thought it would be especially *appropriate*. That was the word he used. Appropriate to meet at the cemetery. And Madd had giggled madly at the thought. That's a joke, sir. One we use all the time.

Of course Willowbrook's gates are closed at night, but that's never stopped us before. It's simple to scale the stone wall. There are chinks between the places where the stones fit that are perfect hand- and footholds. I can show you, if you like.

I strolled down the walkway—number fourteen west. There's no number thirteen, you know. People can be so stupid about things like that. So number fourteen *is* number thirteen. Only it's not called that. Anyway, the path swings down past Colonel Bragdon's large granite monument, the one that says GONE BUT NOT FORGOTTEN,

23

and then around that little stone angel that Madd coos over every time. It's really kind of sappy.

Then you turn right and go down over the hill and on the slope is Agnes's grave.

No, I don't know who first found the place. Or who first had the idea of sitting on the stone. All of us together, I'd guess.

I sat down and waited, pulling a paperback out of my pocket. *A Separate Peace*, if that's important. It's an assignment. About World War II.

The air was crisp but not cold. There'd been a lot of sun and Agnes was a regular little toaster. I'd got about three pages in when I heard a crunching sound—feet on fallen leaves. Looking up, I saw Madd.

"I finished already," she said, meaning the book.

"Any good?" I asked.

"I cried," she said. But then she's an easy crier.

Billy came right behind her and they joined me on the stone.

"Agnes is sure warm tonight!" Madd said.

"She must know it's Halloween," Billy added.

We laughed at that. It was like an ordinary evening at Chez Doubleday. That's French for "Doubleday's house."

We talked on for about fifteen minutes, I'd guess. No, I didn't check my watch, but the Holy Moly Mother church bell rang out the quarter hour. You know—St. Mary's? And I'm sure I'd heard at least one set of ringing since I'd gotten to the graveyard.

And then, oddly, we all shivered simultaneously.

"Someone walking over my grave," said Billy. He says it every time he shivers at Willowbrook. You know—from the cold.

"Me too!" said Madd.

"Me three!" I added.

Then we all looked at one another and laughed.

"Halloween," I said, singing it out.

I mean it was not a big deal. We all thought it was funny, really, that we were in a cemetery that night.

And then a dog behind the keeper's house started howling.

"Trick-or-treaters," said Madd by way of explanation.

"Of course," Billy and I agreed. Only we knew that though the dog's supposed to be a watchdog, he never barks at us when we go over the wall. And now, all of a sudden, he wasn't just barking, he was howling.

"Ghosts," said Madd in a spooky voice. She waggled her fingers at us. "Spooks."

It made us all start laughing again. I mean, none of us believe in ghosts, after all. But our laughter was sort of strained, and Billy's went on much too long and loudly.

Then Madd's face got white. I mean it almost glowed in the gathering dark. Her mouth opened, shut, then opened again.

"Turn around," she said. "Slowly. Tell me what you see." Her voice was very strange.

So Billy and I, who were sitting facing her, turned slowly.

"I see—" Billy began, almost as a joke. Then he stopped. And pointed.

I saw what he was pointing at. Something white floating about five feet off the ground, wavering in the gloom down at the bottom of the hill.

"Toilet paper," I said. "Someone's been out on trick night."

But it wasn't toilet paper. I know because later on I checked.

"A ghost costume? Bedsheets?" asked Madd. But we could see through whatever it was to the trees behind.

Movie camera. Slide projector. SFX. We thought of them all, sir. Honest.

And then the thing started up the hill toward us. Floating. And going really fast.

Billy broke first, running back up to the path and past the howling dog, and on into the street. Madd took another moment before she went, not running but not exactly going slow.

I stayed till the thing came close. I mean *close*. I could see its face—a woman's face, old and white and angry. I had seen that face before somewhere, sir, but I couldn't figure out where.

By then I was so scared, neither of my legs seemed able to move. I was like stone.

The thing floated above me and pointed a bony finger at my head. It mouthed silent words at me. But I could read them. No problem at all.

"Get. Off. My. Stone!" it said.

I got. My legs suddenly able to move on their own accord, I leaped up and went galloping down the hill, past the ghost, and over the wall. I turned to look back once, and I could see the white thing capering on the top of the grave, waving its arms above its head.

And then I remembered where I'd seen that face before. In a portrait hanging up over the entryway in the Doubleday library in town. I worked there last summer as a page. The stories they tell about Mrs. D. are not pretty, sir. But then I guess you know all about them.

No, I don't expect you to believe me, sir. But I do think you should put barbed wire up around the graveyard. And get a better dog for the groundskeeper. I mean, that was one angry lady, sir. And no telling what she'll do next Halloween if there are kids gathering for a quiet talk on her grave. I mean—she was your grandmother, sir. I thought if anyone would understand, it would be you.

The story of the White Lady who walks around the ruined cathedral in St. Andrews, Scotland, is well known in the town. Since St. Andrews is where my husband and I have a summer home, I have often hoped to see her. But alas, not one glimpse! Not in sunshine or at midnight or in the deepest haar, the fog that rolls in grey and thick off the North Sea.

The place where she is supposed to walk is by a tower, in the cathedral's outer walls, that was the burial chamber of the Lairds of Denbrae. In 1868 the tower's upper room was opened up and the coffins were examined. One allegedly contained the embalmed cadaver of a female wearing white leather gloves, with long, still-burnished hair. That exhumation was the start of a popular ghost story, and the sightings have proliferated for a hundred years. The last time she was seen by Scottish een (Scots for "eyes") was in the 1950s, when two young medical students—who swore they had been entirely sober at the time—spotted her walking by the cathedral wall.

The White Lady

She walks at night
All dressed in white,
Her hands in leather gloves,
Around the wall
When night birds call
And mournful coo the doves.

She scares the folk
Who scarce dare joke
About her tower room
Whence come the moans
And ghastly groans
That pierce the Scottish gloom.

She's not been seen
By Scottish *een*
In forty years or more
And only then
By two young men—
Quite sober, this they swore.

Oh I have cased
That famous place;
Her ghost I've tried to raise
In wind and *haar*,
On foot, in car,
And many other ways.

But not one sight
Of ghostly white
Or trailing bit of gown,
Nor glove nor hair
Have I glimpsed there
Within St. Andrews town.

In the late 1970s I was working on a collection of stories for a book called Dream Weaver. *My editor suggested that I needed one more tale, a story about death. Having been a dancer in my youth—studying at George Balanchine's ballet school—I immediately thought of a title, "The Boy Who Danced with Death." But that reminded me too much of a marvelous Peter Beagle short story, "Come, Lady Death," in which Death is a woman at a ball. I didn't want to write anything that similar. So instead, I changed the title to "The Boy Who Sang for Death." Title first, story after. Besides, I used to make money as a folksinger.*

You will see that there are two endings to this story. I did that on purpose. You can choose which one you prefer. You can guess which is my favorite.

As I was reading the draft of the story aloud to myself in our kitchen (I always read my work aloud as I revise), I stumbled over the line: "Any gift I have I would surely give to get my mother back." And I began to cry. To sob, actually. At that moment I realized that on some deep level the story was about me—as so many of my stories turn out to be—and that I was still mourning my own mother, who had died five years earlier. Maybe ghosts are the manifestation of memory. Stories certainly are.

The Boy Who Sang for Death

In a village that lay like a smudge on the cheek of a quiet valley, there lived an old woman and the last of her seven sons. The oldest six had joined the army as they came of age, and her husband was long in his grave. The only one left at home was a lad named Karl.

Even if he had not been her last, his mother would have loved him best, for he had a sweet disposition and a sweeter voice. It was because of that voice, pure and clear, that caroled like spring birds, that she had called him Karel. But his father and brothers, fearing

31

the song name would unman him, had changed it to Karl. So Karl he had remained.

Karl was a sturdy boy, a farm boy in face and hands. But his voice set him apart from the rest. Untutored and untrained, Karl's voice could call home sheep from the pasture, birds from the trees. In the village, it was even said that the sound of Karl's voice made greybeards dance and the lame to walk. Yet Karl used his voice for no such magic, but to please his mother and gentle his flock.

One day when Karl was out singing to the sheep and goats to bring them safely in from the field, his voice broke; like a piece of cloth caught on a nail, it tore. Fearing something wrong at home, he hurried the beasts. They scattered before him, and he came to the house to find that his mother had died.

"Between one breath and the next, she was gone," said the priest.

Gently Karl folded her hands on her breast and, although she was beyond the sound of his song, he whispered something in her ear and turned to leave.

"Where are you going?" called out the priest, his words heavy with concern.

"I am going to find Death and bring my mother back," cried Karl, his jagged voice now dulled with grief. He turned at the door and faced the priest who knelt by his mother's bed. "Surely Death will accept an exchange. What is one old, tired woman to Death, who has known so many?"

"And will you recognize Death, my son, when you meet him?"

"That I do not know," said Karl.

The priest nodded and rose heavily from his knees. "Then listen well, my son. Death is an aging but still handsome prince. His eyes are dark and empty, for he has seen much suffering in the world. If you find such a one, he is Death."

"I will know him," said Karl.

"And what can you give Death in exchange that he has not already had many times over?" asked the priest.

Karl touched his pockets and sighed. "I have nothing here to give," he said. "But I hope that he may listen to my songs. They tell me in the village that there is a gift of magic in my voice. Any gift I have I would surely give to get my mother back. I will sing for Death, and perhaps that great prince will take time to listen."

"Death does not take time," said the old priest, raising his hand to bless the boy, "for time is Death's own greatest possession."

"I can but try," said Karl, tears in his eyes. He knelt a moment for the blessing, stood up, and went out the door. He did not look back.

Karl walked for many days and came at last to a city that lay like a blemish on three hills. He listened quietly but well, as only a singer can, and when he heard weeping, he followed the sound and found a funeral procession bearing the coffin of a child. The procession turned into a graveyard where stones leaned upon stones like cards in a neglected deck.

"Has Death been here already?" asked Karl of a weeping woman.

"Death has been here many times," she answered. "But today she has taken my child."

"She?" said Karl. "But surely Death is a man."

"Death is a woman," she answered him at once. "Her hair is long and thick and dark, like the roots of trees. Her body is huge and brown, but she is barren. The only way she can bear a child is to bear it away."

Karl felt her anger and sorrow then, for they matched his own, so he joined the line of mourners to the grave. And when the child's tiny box had been laid in the ground, he sang it down with the others. But his voice lifted above theirs, a small bird soaring with

33

ease over larger ones. The townsfolk stopped singing, in amazement, and listened to him.

Karl sang not of death but of his village in the valley, of the seasons that sometimes stumble one into another, and of the small pleasures of the hearth. He sang tune after tune the whole of that day, and just at nightfall he stopped. They threw dirt on the baby's coffin and brought Karl to their home.

"Your songs eased my little one's passage," said the woman. "Stay with us this night. We owe you that."

"I wish that I had been here before," said Karl. "I might have saved your baby with a song."

"I fear Death would not be cheated so easily of her chosen child," said the woman. She set the table but did not eat.

Karl left in the morning. And as he walked, he thought about Death, how it was a hollow-eyed prince to the priest but a jealous mother to the woman. If Death could change shapes with such ease, how would he know Death when they finally met? He walked and walked, his mind in a puzzle, until he came at last to a plain that lay like a great open wound between mountains.

The plain was filled with an army of fighting men. There were men with bows and men with swords and men with wooden staves. Some men fought on horseback, and some fought from their knees. Karl could not tell one band of men from another, could not match friend with friend, foe with foe, for their clothes were colored by dirt and by blood and every man looked the same. And the screams and shouts and the crying of horns were a horrible symphony in Karl's ears.

Yet there was one figure Karl *could* distinguish. A woman, quite young, dressed in a long, white gown. Her dark braids were caught up in ribbons of white and looped like a crown on her head. She threaded her way through the ranks of men like a shuttle through a

loom, and there seemed to be a pattern in her going. She paused now and then to put a hand to the head or the breast of one man and then another. Each man she touched stopped fighting and, with an expression of surprise, left his body and followed the girl, so that soon there was a great wavering line of grey men trailing behind her.

Then Karl knew that he had found Death.

He ran down the mountainside and around the flank of the great plain, for he wanted to come upon Death face to face. He called out as he ran, hoping to slow her progress. "Wait, oh, wait, my Lady Death, please wait for me."

Lady Death heard his call above the battle noise, and she looked up from her work. A weariness sat between her eyes, but she did not stop. She continued her way from man to man, a hand to the brow or over the heart. And at her touch, each man left his life to follow the young girl named Death.

When Karl saw that she would not stop at his calling, he stepped into her path. But she walked through him as if through air and went on her way, threading the line of dead grey men behind her.

So Karl began to sing. It was all he knew to do.

He sang not of death but of growing and bearing, for they were things she knew nothing of. He sang of small birds on the apple spray and bees with their honeyed burden. He sang of the first green blades piercing the warmed earth. He sang of winter fields where moles and mice sleep quietly under the snow. Each tune swelled into the next.

And Lady Death stopped to listen.

As she stopped, the ribbon of soldiers that was woven behind her stopped, too, and from their dead eyes tears fell with each memory. The battlefield was still, frozen by the songs. And the only sound and the only movement and the only breath was Karl's voice.

When he had finished at last, a tiny brown bird flew out of a dead tree, took up the last melody, and went on.

"I have made you stop, Lady Death," cried Karl. "And you have listened to my tunes. Will you now pay for that pleasure?"

Lady Death smiled, a slow, weary smile, and Karl wondered that someone so young should have to carry such a burden. And his pity hovered between them in the quiet air.

"I will pay, Karel," she said.

He did not wonder that she knew his true name, for Lady Death would, in the end, know every human's name.

"Then I ask for my mother in exchange," said Karl.

Lady Death looked at him softly then. She took up his pity and gave it back. "That I cannot do. Who follows me once, follows forever. But is it not payment enough to know that you have stayed my hand for this hour? No man has ever done that before."

"But you promised to pay," said Karl. His voice held both anger and disappointment, a man and a child's voice in one.

"And what I promise," she said, looking at him from under darkened lids, "I do."

Ending 1

Lady Death put her hand in front of her, as if reaching into a cupboard, and a grey form that was strangely transparent took shape under her fingers. It became a harp, with smoke-colored strings the color of Lady Death's eyes.

"A useless gift," said Karl. "I cannot play."

But Lady Death reached over and set the harp in his hand, careful not to touch him with her own.

And as the harp molded itself under his fingers, Karl felt music surge through his bones. He put his thumb and forefinger on the strings and began to play.

At the first note, the battle began anew. Men fought, men bled,

37

men suffered, men fell. But Karl passed through the armies untouched, playing a sweet tune that rose upward, in bursts, as the lark and its song spring toward the sun. He walked through the armies, through the battle, through the plain, playing his harp, and he never looked back again.

Ending 2

"And what I promise," Death said, looking at him from under darkened lids, "I do."

She turned and pointed to the field, and Karl's eyes followed her fingers.

"There in that field are six men whose heads and hearts I will not touch this day. Look carefully, Karel."

He looked. "They are my brothers," he said.

"Them, I will spare." And Lady Death turned and stared into Karl's face with her smoky eyes. "But I would have you sing for me again each night in the small hours when I rest, for I have never had such comfort before. Will you come?" She held out her hand.

Karl hesitated a moment, remembering his farm, remembering the fields, the valleys, the warm spring rains. Then he looked again at Lady Death, whose smile seemed a little less weary. He nodded and reached for her hand, and it was small and soft and cool in his. He raised her hand once to his lips, then set it, palm open, over his heart. He never felt the cold.

Then, hand in hand, Karl and Lady Death walked through the battlefield. Their passing made not even the slightest breeze on the cheeks of the wounded, nor an extra breath for the dying. Only the dead who traveled behind saw them pass under the shadows of the farthest hills. But long after they had gone, the little bird sang Karl's last song over and over and over again into the darkening air.

At the dawning of the nineteenth century in England and America, ghost stories were popular with the literary set. At the same time, folklore studies were beginning in earnest. By the end of the century there was a growing interest in psychic phenomenon, including ghosts. Seances became the rage. A seance is usually run by a person known as a medium. The object is to call up a ghostly spirit or spirits. Of course the seances were all fake—or were they?

I wrote this poem after seeing the movie Ghost *for the umpteenth time. Whoopi Goldberg plays a medium who knows she is a fake until she actually calls up a spirit, played by Patrick Swayze. If I could be sure of calling up Patrick Swayze, I'd be a medium, too!*

Seance for Eight

We were eight around the table,
With the lamps turned low,
And we waited while the medium
Began her ghostly show.

She had had us place our fingers
Lightly on the tabletop,
And she warned no matter what occurred
That we must never stop.

Then she closed her eyes and muttered.
"It's a trance," said cousin Jim.
So I rolled *my* eyes and whispered,
"Do you think that we're all dim?"

And from some place very near us
Came the ticking of a clock.
A soft wind arose from nowhere,
Followed quickly by a knock.

Then the table started trembling;
Then the floor began to shake.
I was thinking rather hard that
It was time to take a break.

But before I got myself up
And could head out of the door
Something very weird and wavy
Manifested from the floor.

It was protoplasmic proper
With a long and lingering tail.
It set all eight hearts a-pounding
With its spectral-sounding wail.

And I know that I was screaming
As I leaped onto my feet,
When my little sister Mary
Pulled away the ghostly sheet.

"It's a hoax!" she cried. "A fake thing!"
In quite loud and ringing tones.
But just then beneath the sheeting
We all saw the twitching bones.

41

Bruce Coville called and asked me to write a story for a ghost anthology he was putting together. By the time I hung up, I already had a glimmer of an idea. But it was weeks before I could start to write it. Sometimes life simply takes you by the throat.

I have put a number of personal tidbits in the story. For example, I graduated from a wonderful high school—Staples High in Westport, Connecticut—that had a very strong music program. The choir and chorus were known across the country. I was one of the second altos, occasionally singing tenor when there weren't enough boys who would admit to high voices. We sang the Hallelujah Chorus every Christmas. I fully believe that my choir director would have returned from the grave if that particular piece of music had been dropped by his successor!

Mrs. Ambroseworthy

Specter.
Spook.
Phantom.
Phantasm.
Wraith.
Shadow.
Fetch.
Shade.

Those are all names for a ghost. I know. I checked in the thesaurus. But what I saw coming home from school choir practice didn't look a thing like any of those. You know—misty white and rattling chains. Or skeleton thin like the walking dead. Or gibbering. Or drooling.

What I saw was the ghost of Mrs. Ambroseworthy, our old choir director, the one who was drowned in the boating accident.

She was wringing her hair and muttering. She was not a happy lady.

Not that she'd been especially happy alive. She'd always been upset by Allen's high E or Melanie's low B or the altos coming in a beat too soon or the tenors a beat too late. She got mad when we missed a practice or when practice got canceled on account of a big basketball game. (The tenors were the basketball team, plus one bass.)

But I had never seen her so angry as I did a full five months after her body had washed ashore after the Fourth of July picnic at the lake.

"Mrs. Ambrose—" was all I got out of my mouth before sense and fear combined to silence me. But it was enough. She looked up and shook her finger at me, just as she used to when I sang out on the final rest, the one in the *Hallelujah Chorus.* "Gordon Wilson!" she said, only not aloud. Her mouth said the name and my memory supplied the sound. Mrs. Ambroseworthy had a voice hard to forget, both sharp and musical at the same time, sort of like a handsaw played in a band.

I turned and ran. I am not proud of that. But I'd been afraid of Mrs. Ambroseworthy when she was alive. Dead didn't make her any better.

Now ever since Mrs. Ambroseworthy's unfortunate death—*unfortunate* being my mother's word for it, not mine—Nancy Chapperel has led the choir. She's not much of a musician, but the entire football team now sings. They are, not surprisingly, all basses except for the quarterback. He can afford to be a tenor. Actually, at least nine of them aren't really basses, but Ms. Chapperel lets them stay there anyway. Two of them aren't anything at all—bass, tenor, alto, *or* soprano—but she lets them sing as well.

Ms. Chapperel has long red hair that springs up around her face like a helmet, and a 150-watt smile. She doesn't seem to notice when someone hits a note from the bottom up instead of from the top down. And she even has us singing a Christmas rap that she wrote herself, something Mrs. Ambroseworthy would spin in her grave about. If she *was* in her grave, which I doubted. Actually, the rap is truly stupid:

> *Here comes Santa in a two-ton semi,*
> *Pedal to the metal, wha-wha and whammy,*
> *Whammy, whammy, wha-wha-whammy....*

The backfield really likes that one. They were so rough on the *Hallelujah Chorus,* we had to drop it from the program. Which is too bad, since it was kind of a tradition. You know—once is a tryout, twice is a repeat, and three times is a tradition? Still, it's the first time so many upperclassmen have been part of the school choir, so no one is complaining. Especially not a middle schooler like me.

But a ghost haunting the path behind First Baptist wasn't right. It wasn't comforting, either. I wondered what had caused Mrs. Ambroseworthy to come back now, almost half a year after her drowning.

Of course I didn't bother to do any of this wondering until I was safely home with the door locked and Mom's best garlic powder ground into the floor around my bed. Mrs. Ambroseworthy might have been some kind of bloodsucker, you know, disguised. I saw that in a movie on late-night TV. A guy can't be too careful.

Two days later, two nights of choir practice later, and the day before our Christmas performance, I was waiting for someone else to mention seeing Mrs. Ambroseworthy's wet ghost. She hadn't done anything to me but waggle her finger, but it wasn't like she was hiding or anything. She was simply out there on the path, in that old floral print dress, the one that Dad said made her look like she'd been upholstered rather than dressed. I'm not making this up, you know. She was definitely there. The ground underneath her was soaking wet. Yet for all that there were forty-seven kids in the choir (up from thirty last year because of the football team), no one said a thing.

Maybe, like me, they were afraid of being called cowards. Maybe, like me, they were afraid they were going crazy.

So I decided to broach the subject—that's what my mom calls it when you kind of sneak up on something backward without actually committing yourself—during the Kool-Aid break in the vestry. We practice at the First Baptist Church because that's where we perform. It has an organ, a piano, and enough seats, which our school does not.

"So," I said, loud enough for at least half the tenors and all of the girls to hear me, "anyone here believe in ghosts?"

Three of the girls, including Tammie Lee, giggled. Tammie Lee put her hand over her mouth to do it. Her fingernails were like little pearls. Jimmy Stearnes punched me in the arm.

"Sure," he said. "And UFOs, too. Woo-woo!"

"I don't," I hastened to add. "Believe in ghosts, I mean." So much for broaching. "But I just wondered if someone here did?"

Lindsey Windsor—who we called Lady because she always wore dresses—raised her hand. Just like she wanted to be excused to go to the bathroom or something. "I do," she said, her face all scrunched up with the thought.

Just what I needed. Help from Lady.

"I do," she repeated, only in a very small voice. Lady Windsor always speaks in this tiny little voice so you have to lean toward her to hear what she's saying. Except when she sings. Then she has this incredibly pure soprano that simply soars over all the rest. She used to get all the solos B.C.—Before Chapperel, that is. It's hard to be a soprano singing rap. And the one soprano solo this year, in "O Holy Night," was transposed for the quarterback as a reward for admitting he was a tenor. Jack Armstrong. I kid you not. (Well, actually, his name is Geoffrey. Geoff Armstrong. But everyone calls him Jack the All-American Boy. And he did make All State in two sports.) He's the same guy who said, "Pitch is for wimps." And he didn't mean baseball.

"I do," Lady Windsor said again in her tiny voice, the voice that has been one seat behind me ever since first grade, Windsor coming right after Wilson. "I saw one."

"Saw one what?" I asked.

"She saw a ghost, a ghouly ghost," sang Tammie Lee. Then she giggled again, pearl-fingered hand to mouth. She looked like an oyster. The other girls giggled along with her. Sometimes I hate girls. Or maybe, as Mom says, I'm just not ready for them.

"It was Mrs. Ambroseworthy," Lady said.

The entire section leaned toward her, then leaned back, roaring with laughter. Forty-six kids roared altogether. That's forty-five plus me. I roared, too. I am not proud of that. I am pretty sure I was the only one who shouldn't have been laughing.

Lady Windsor's face scrunched up some more and got shiny with tears. Then she ran out of the vestry and up the stairs. We could hear her feet running up the aisles and then the great *screak* of the front door opening and the *slam* of it closing after.

"I guess we weren't very nice," I said, only not real loud.

"Mrs. Ambroseworthy..." Jack Armstrong said slowly. "The old choir director?" He may be All State, but he's not All Smart.

"She drowned last summer," Tammie Lee said, fluttering at him. "It was an accident."

"Accident," the bass section suddenly boomed in. "Ax, ax, accident." Like it was a new song.

"Not an ax, you yo-yos," I muttered. "A boat." But I said it very softly.

Just then Ms. Chapperel came in from the minister's office, where she'd been working on some additional lyrics to the rap. She handed them out. "I can tell you are eager, kids," she said. "So let's go. And—oh—did I hear somebody leave?" She watted her smile at us. Cute. Definitely cute.

Jack Armstrong was first as always. "Just Lady Windsor," he said. "Why? Was she feeling ill?"

"I don't have a *ghost* of an idea," Jack said. Everyone laughed. Even me. I am especially not proud of *that*.

For a two-letter man, Armstrong is occasionally fast on his feet. And clumsy on everyone else's.

We struggled through the new lyrics. After all, we had only one night to learn them.

> *Bringing to the good kids stockings full of candy,*
> *Soda pop and lemon drop and everything dandy,*
> *Dandy, dandy, dan-dan-dandy.*

I didn't say Ms. Chapperel was a good writer. It didn't stop the entire bass section from grinning every time she lifted her arms for the downbeat.

The boys in the back row were hip-hopping to the music, and the risers began to shake. Ms. Chapperel had to caution them a couple of times. But as we plowed through the rest of the new verses, I almost hoped the whole place would collapse. The *Hallelujah Chorus* was looking awfully good in retrospect. Memory does that. Especially when memory has to contend with *these* lyrics.

Eventually choir practice was over, and we had to go home. It's a small town, and most of us walked. Even the upperclassmen. It's hard to convince your dad to lend you the car for the evening when First Baptist is right down the block.

Only Lady and I actually live behind the church, which means cutting through a backyard, through the old cemetery, and then on through Evers Copse, a silly name for a small if ancient stand of trees. Some Evers or other has always owned it. Of course we kids called it Every Cops, because every cop in town hides at the far end of it to catch speeders.

I would have walked the long way home, avoiding the yard and the cemetery, but it was an extra forty minutes because of the superhighway and the swinging bridge and all. In the end I'd have to go through the copse anyway. And that's where Mrs. Ambroseworthy's ghost waited. Why there? I didn't know. My only other option was to stay all night in the church. My parents, of course, would have had a fit and, I suspect, around midnight would have had the police to First Baptist. I could have lived with that. But before I knew it, Ms. Chapperel had shooed us all out and sent us scattering away home, giving off that 150-watt grin and calling out, "Sleep well, kids. Tomorrow will be great."

So, dragging my feet, I went through the yard and straight into the cemetery. It had never been a scary place for us kids. We picnic there all the time. I checked Mrs. Ambroseworthy's grave, and it was undisturbed, though someone had put plastic flowers in a metal holder in front of it. The bright pink flowers looked odd against the snow.

There was nothing for it. I had to go through the copse. I took a deep breath and started.

And then I heard it. The crying. Loud and soft and loud again.

"Who's . . . who's there?" I called out.

"Gordon?" There was a sob at the end of it. I could barely hear my name.

"Lady?"

"Lindsey." (Sniff.) "I hate being called Lady." (Fade out.) Something white and fluttery started toward me, but it was only Lady . . . er, Lindsey's scarf.

"I've been waiting and waiting till you got here. And I'm awfully cold. But I just couldn't go through the trees on my own."

"Because of . . ." I asked.

"Because of . . ." She nodded.

Somehow it was even scarier not mentioning Mrs. Ambroseworthy's name.

"Why is she here, Gordon?"

I began to say "How should I know?" when the ghost suddenly appeared about ten feet away, as wet as ever, and wringing her hair. After about ten silent wrings, she turned and looked at us. Her eyes weren't red and shiny. She didn't have fangs or long nails. She didn't need them. She was scary enough on her own.

I found that my tongue had stuck to the roof of my mouth, like it was superglued there. I couldn't have spoken even if I had wanted to. But Lindsey surprised me. Grabbing my hand and squeezing it for courage, she said in her tiny, quiet voice, "What do you want, Mrs. Ambroseworthy?"

Of course the ghost had to float a whole lot closer to hear her,

49

and I just about passed out, but Lindsey kept holding on to my hand so I couldn't go anywhere.

I added my voice to Lindsey's. "What *do* you want?" My tongue was floppy in my mouth.

The ghost stared at the two of us and pointed her left forefinger up in the air, then pushed it higher and higher, the way she used to when anyone was flat. Usually me.

"You want me to sing higher?" Suddenly I had a quiver in my voice.

The ghost shook her head and water splashed everywhere, but none of it landed on us.

"You want to go up?" I asked. This time my voice was almost strong. "Like to Heaven?"

"Only you can't?" Lindsey whispered. I squeezed her hand back.

The ghost nodded.

"Can we help?" we asked together.

Mrs. Ambroseworthy's ghost smiled, the same smile I had seen only once before, near the end of Lindsey's solo in "O Holy Night" when she hit that high note and held it, clear and pure and beautiful and long, long past the rest of us straggling behind her in harmony.

The night of the concert was one of those crisp, cold nights in December that make you think of Christmas cards. My mom and dad and little sister and I walked together to First Baptist. Dad held Mom's hand. I went on a little ahead so no one could know we were together.

The vestry was crowded with kids, all of us wearing white shirts or blouses because that's what looks best under the choir robes. Except for Jack Armstrong, whose shirt was more cream colored.

"Because I've got the solo!" he said brightly. But his own color wasn't all that good. On his face, I mean. He was probably thinking about pitch. Mrs. Ambroseworthy had always cautioned soloists not to think too much before a performance. Just practice.

We filed onto the risers, and Ms. Chapperel stood up in her tight black dress and walked toward us. The audience applauded and the basses nudged one another, grinning.

We already knew the order of things. First a series of seven favorite Christmas carols, then a medley of pop Christmas tunes, like "I Saw Mommy Kissing Santa Claus" and "Jingle-Bell Rock." (I didn't say they were modern, just pop.) Then a break for juice, three Chanukah songs as a nod to multiculturalists, the rap song, and last, "O Holy Night," with Jack's solo. Just to be sure we remembered the new words for the rap, Ms. Chapperel had made large cue cards that stood on an easel facing us.

The carols went all right. They were old standbys, and those of us who had been in choir before had sung them all with Mrs. Ambroseworthy. If we were a bit ragged, it was because Ms. Chapperel was as nervous as we were, and hesitated once or twice on an upbeat. But I expect the only ones who noticed were Lindsey and me.

And Mrs. Ambroseworthy.

She stood in the back of the hall, behind a pillar, so no one could see her. But I spotted the puddle as it widened and deepened and began to creep down the aisle.

The pop tunes weren't too bad, either, though the tenors missed their entrance on "Jingle-Bell Rock" and the sopranos overpowered everyone on "All I Want for Christmas Is My Two Front Teeth."

Lindsey and I scarcely sang a note, and both the tenor and soprano sections sorely missed our direction. We were waiting, you see.

After intermission—and the church janitor *tsk-tsk*ing over the puddle and putting out a bucket because he thought melting snow had come through the roof—we climbed back onto the risers. Mrs. Ambroseworthy had disappeared, so nobody had seen her. My mom had twice wiped my face with her handkerchief, thinking I was sweating because of the concert, and I had almost been overwhelmed by the scent.

Lindsey looked at me and nodded. I nodded back. Sam Dougal noticed and elbowed me.

"Sweet on Lady?" he asked.

I stepped on his instep. Hard. It made him squeak out loud, and that brought a sharp look from Ms. Chapperel at the tenor section. Jack Armstrong was so nervous, he thought it was a look meant for him and stepped forward for his solo.

"Not *now!*" hissed Ms. Chapperel.

Jack turned beet red and stepped back up on the riser. He was shaking.

Now! I thought. *Mrs. Ambroseworthy. Now!*

But she didn't appear. The piano accompaniment began, and we plowed through Chanukah and launched into the rap.

"Here comes Santa," chanted the sopranos, the basses adding: "In a two-ton semi."

And *then* Mrs. Ambroseworthy stepped into view, behind the last rows. No one in the audience could see her, of course, as they were all looking at the choir. But she was fully visible to all of us kids.

The tenors got as far as "Pedal to the . . ." and then all the old members suddenly *really* noticed her. How could they not? She was wringing the water out of her hair.

They sang: "Puddle, puddle, pud-pud-puddle . . ." Then they quietly panicked and stopped singing altogether. Ginger Martin and Todd Benton began to moan, and Mary Martin McGee crossed herself three times and said a number of quick prayers never heard before at First Baptist. That left the football team, some of whom didn't recognize Mrs. Ambroseworthy and probably thought she was some-body's wet old aunt who had come in late. They kept struggling along with the song on their own. Of course, without the *real* singers, they just sounded like a bunch of monotones doing karaoke—which, in a way, they were.

The audience began to mutter.

Ms. Chapperel worked hard to pull us together, I'll say that for her. But when Ginger pointed and Ms. Chapperel turned around to see what was making Ginger gibber, the ghost disappeared—except for the puddle. So the choir began to straggle back onto the notes that the piano accompanist had doggedly kept playing. We forgot to do the extra lyrics, though, and Ms. Chapperel's 150-watt grin was gone as if a circuit breaker had been thrown.

And we still had one song to go, the song Lindsey and Mrs. Ambroseworthy and I had planned on. The one that would carry our old choir director to her perfect rest.

Ms. Chapperel signaled to Jack. "Now!" she whispered, clearly having decided she'd had a moment's weakness. Her grin was back in place. "Now!"

But Jack could not move. After all, he had recognized Mrs. Ambroseworthy. Though he'd never been in the choir before, he'd known her well. It had been his dad's boat she'd fallen out of before she drowned. Nervous about the solo to begin with, he was now as white as . . . well, as a ghost. Or as ghosts *should* be if they aren't Mrs. Ambroseworthy.

"Jack!" Ms. Chapperel stage-whispered.

This time he stepped forward, like a robot, and I was right behind him, a shadow, a shade, a wraith.

The piano began its arpeggios, up and down and up again, and just then Mrs. Ambroseworthy reappeared, her arms high above her head.

53

I tapped Jack on the shoulder and whispered, "Boo!"

He passed out and I caught him smoothly. From the front it looked as if I was a hero, catching him like that.

Lindsey stepped forward and sailed right into Jack's solo without missing a beat. Only—and this was unusual for her—she was slightly flat. Must have been nerves, from the rap and the ghost and all.

Ms. Chapperel sure didn't notice. She was just glad to get us all singing again. But we were ragged and Lindsey was flat. Mrs. Ambroseworthy, alive or dead, would never stand for that. And she didn't, either. She moved silently, swiftly, wetly, to right behind Ms. Chapperel, waving her own arms to get us back on beat.

I thought the audience would faint on the spot.

Then Mrs. Ambroseworthy lifted that warning finger and pointed to the ceiling. "Higher!" her voice hissed in my head.

Lindsey's shoulders suddenly straightened, as if she, too, had heard Mrs. Ambroseworthy's voice, and suddenly her soprano soared right on to the perfect pitch, hitting it from the top down. And stayed there.

"Higher!" Mrs. Ambroseworthy said again in my mind, stabbing her finger into the air. And as I watched, she floated, smiling, as sure as Lindsey's voice, up and up and up and up, heading for the ceiling of First Baptist and beyond.

We got a new choir director the next year, one who knew music and reinstated the *Hallelujah Chorus*, which I sang without a single mistake. Ms. Chapperel ran off to marry the coach of the college football team. Lindsey filled out, her voice got stronger, she forgave me all my instances of cowardice, and we have been going steady ever since.

But that's another story altogether.

All-all-altogether.

I really was frightened of wolves under my bed and a bear in my closet when I was a child living in New York City. In fact I was so frightened, I didn't dare get out of bed—even to go to the toilet—until first light. One night I just couldn't wait until dawn. Leaping from my bed, I managed to get into the hall without hitting the floor once. Dashing to the bathroom, I slammed the door behind me. Blessed relief. But then I realized in horror that I could not get safely back to my bed. So I curled up in the tub, two folded towels for a pillow, and slept there until morning.

I originally published this story in an anthology called Haunted House, *but am delighted to find another place for it. The rest of this story may come from my imagination, but not those wolves or that bear! Perhaps this story is an exorcism, a kind of coin on the dead eyes of my past. I certainly don't fear night wolves anymore.*

Night Wolves

When we moved into the old house on Brown's End, I knew the night wolves would move with us. And the bear. They had lived in every bedroom I'd ever had—the one in Allentown and the one in Phoenix and the one in Westport.

The wolves lived under my bed, the bear in my closet. They only came out at night.

I knew—I *absolutely* knew—that if I got out of bed in the middle of the night, I was a goner. You couldn't begin to imagine how big that bear was or how many teeth those wolves had. You couldn't imagine. But I could.

So I put the bear trap I had made out of Legos and paper clips in front of the closet. And I put the wolf trap I had built out of my brother Jensen's broken pocketknife and the old Christmas tree stand at the foot of my bed. And I kept the night-light on, even though I was ten when we moved to Brown's End.

That meant, of course, that no one dared come into my room in the dark, not Mom or Jensen, or even Dad, though we rarely saw him since he got married to Kate. And none of my friends stayed overnight.

It was safer that way.

Of course the minute it got to be light outside, the wolves and bear disappeared. I never did figure out where they went. And then I could go to the bathroom. Or get a new book from my bookcase. Or sit on the floor to put on my socks. Or anything.

Which meant winters were tough, especially now that we were living in the north, the dawn coming so late and all.

In Phoenix once, when I was eight, I was sick to my stomach and I just *had* to go to the bathroom. I waited and waited until it was almost too late, then made a dash over the foot of my bed. I managed to get out of the room in one big leap, my heart pounding so loud it sounded like I had a rock band inside. But I had to spend the rest of the night curled up in the tub because I could hear the wolves sniffing and snuffling around the bathroom door.

So when we moved to Brown's End without my dad, I expected the wolves and the bear. I just didn't expect the ghost.

I heard it on the very first night, a kind of low sobbing: *ooh-wooo-ooooooooo*.

The wolves heard it, too, and it made them nervous. They rushed around under my bed, growling and scratching all night, trying to get past the trap.

The next night the bear heard it, too. He thrashed around so in the closet that when dawn came and I opened the closet door, my best sweater and my confirmation suit had fallen to the floor.

But the third night, the low sobbing turned into a cry that came

57

from across the hall in the room where my mom slept. And then I was *really* scared.

"Mom!" I called out. I usually don't like to do that for fear of reminding the wolves and bear that I am in the room with them. Then a little louder I called out, "Mom?"

She didn't wake up and call back that everything was all right.

So then I did something I *never* do. I called to Jensen, who was in the next room. Ever since Phoenix we've had our own rooms. I hated to do that because he always teases me anyway, calling me a baby for needing a night-light. A baby! He's only eleven himself.

But Jensen didn't wake up, either. In fact I could hear him snoring. If I could only snore like that, I bet there wouldn't be any wolves or bear around my room.

I tried to sleep, but the ghost's sobbing came again.

I put the pillow over my head but somehow that made it worse.

I stayed that way until dawn. I didn't sleep much.

"Do you suppose this house is haunted?" I asked at breakfast, before we headed off to our new school.

Jensen snorted into his cereal. But Mom put her head to one side and considered me for a long while.

"Yeah, haunted," Jensen said. "By the ghosts of wolves. And a big ugly closet bear." I had made the mistake of telling the family about them when I was littler. And back when we were a family. Dad had teased me—and so had Jensen.

"Jensen..." Mom warned.

So I didn't bring it up again. Not at breakfast and not at dinner, either. But when we went to bed that night, I borrowed two pieces of cotton from Mom's dresser and stuck them in my ears. Then I brushed my teeth, went to the bathroom, and jumped into bed. It's when I hit the bed the first time at night that the wolves know it's time to wake up. And the bear.

Mom came in and kissed me good night. She turned on the night-light and turned off the overhead.

"Leave the door open," I reminded her. Not that she ever needed reminding.

And I lay down and quickly fell asleep.

It was well past midnight that I woke. The wolves and bear were quiet. It was the ghost sobbing loudly in Mom's room that woke me. I was surprised it hadn't wakened her. But then she doesn't hear the wolves or bear, either. She says that since I do, I'm a hero every time I get into bed. I know I'm no hero—but I'd sure like to be.

The ghost went on and on and I began to wonder if it were dangerous. Bad enough that Dad was gone. If anything should happen to Mom . . .

I thought about that for a long time. After all, the foot of my bed was even closer to the door than it had been in Phoenix. And I was bigger.

I pulled the cotton out of my ears. The sound of the crying was so loud, the house seemed to shake with it. How could *anyone* sleep through that racket? I sat up in bed and the wolves began to growl. The bear pushed the closet door open, which squeaked a little in protest, inching out against the trap.

Ohowwwwwwwwwoooooooooo.

And then Mom's voice came, only terribly muffled. "Pete!" she cried. My name. And my Dad's.

Only Dad wasn't there.

That's when I knew that wolves and bear or no—I had to help her. I was her only hope.

"Get back, you suckers!" I shouted at the wolves, and threw the cotton balls down. They landed softly on the floor by the bed and muzzled the wolves.

"Leave me alone, you big overgrown rug!" I called to the bear, flinging my pillow at the closet door. The pillow thudded against the door, jamming it.

Without thinking it through any further than that, I jumped from the bed foot and landed, running through the doorway. Two steps brought me into my mom's room.

That was when I saw it—the ghost—hovering over her bed. It was all in white, a slim female ghost in a long dress and a white veil. She was crying and crying.

"Why..." I said, my voice shaking, "why are you here? Who are you?"

The ghost turned toward me and slowly lifted her veil. I shivered, expecting to see maybe a shining skull with dark eye sockets or a monster with weeping sores or—I don't know—maybe even a wolf's head. But what I saw was like a faded familiar photograph. It took me a moment to understand. And then I knew—the ghost wore my mother's face, my mother's wedding dress. She was young and slim and...beautiful.

Behind me in my room, the wolves had set up an awful racket. The bear had joined in snuffling and snorting. When I looked I could see red eyes glaring at me at the door's edge.

The ghost caught her breath and shivered.

"It's all right," I said. "They won't hurt us. Not here." I put my hand out to her. "And don't be sad. If you hadn't gotten married, where would I be? Or Jensen?"

The ghost looked at me for a long moment, considering, then lowered the veil.

"Pete? Honey?" My mom's voice came from the bed, sleepy yet full of wonder. "What are you doing in my room?"

"Being a hero, I guess," I said to her and to the wedding ghost and to myself. "You were having an awful bad dream."

"Not a bad dream, sweetie. A sad dream," she said. "And then I remembered I had you and your brother, and it was all happy again. Do you want me to walk you back to your room?"

I looked over at the doorway. The red eyes were gone. "Nah," I said. "Who's afraid of a couple of night wolves and an old bear anyway? That's kid stuff." I kissed her on the cheek and watched as the ghost faded into the first rays of dawn. "I think I'm gonna like it here, Mom."

I marched back into my room and picked up the trap from the foot of my bed, then the one from in front of the closet door. I heard whimpers, like a litter of puppies, coming from under the bed. I heard a big snore from the closet. I smiled. "I'm gonna like it here a lot."

About ten years ago there were a lot of stories in newspapers and magazines about how flowers, vegetables, and fruit respond to the human voice. "Sing to your plants!" was the popular slogan. As I do not have a green thumb (the phrase used for someone who can grow things easily) but rather a brown one, I found the information fascinating. My plants never flourish. Most die within weeks of my bringing them home. Perhaps, I thought, I could talk them to life.

So I began to speak to my plants, the one straggling Christmas cactus hanging over my cutting board that regularly manages a couple of blossoms on Valentine's Day, the cactus sitting on my kitchen windowsill, and the unnamed bit of green hanging in the window.

What happened? The cactus on the sill died. The other two plants continue their feeble existence.

Maybe, like the hero in this story, I should have sung to them. But look where that gets him.

The Singer of Seeds

There was once a minstrel named Floren who had never held a piece of earth in his hand. He could sing birds out of the trees and milk from a maiden's breast, but of the strong brown soil he knew nothing.

One day, when he came into a small fertile valley named Plaisant and heard the surrounding mountains sing his name, he was more than a little surprised. Still, being a man who believed in signs, he sold his harp for a plow and a plot of land—a poor plow and a strip of earth running close by the mountain foot—and sowed the field.

No one thought he had a hope of a crop, but his strip of land

soon began to sprout. He walked up and down the rows singing to
his grain, and this was his song:

> *Sunlight and moonbright*
> *And wind through the weeds.*
> *Come up and come over,*
> *Come up and come over,*
> *Come up and come over*
> *My swift-growing seeds.*

At first the neighboring farmers had laughed at Floren and his
strange songs. They knew him to be a minstrel, and a good one. He
had entertained at their fairs. But he was not a man of the land. His
father's father's father had not put in long sweaty years at the plow.
So they mocked him, even to his face, and called him Singer of
Seeds.

Floren had returned their mockery with a smile, for even he was
amused at the dirt under his nails and the way the grain seemed to
spring up under his feet. He expected—as they all did—that the
few rows would give him no real harvest and that by winter's edge
he would be singing in their houses for food. Still, the mountain had
called to him and it would have been impolite not to have answered.
So he walked the rows of small tender shoots and sang:

> *"Sunlight and moonbright*
> *And wind through the weeds.*
> *Come up and come over,*
> *Come up and come over,*
> *Come up and come over*
> *My swift-growing seeds."*

After a while he found he loved the sound of his song in the open air, the way it fell against the mountainside and returned to him, the way it seemed to rain down on the new young leaves. After a while, he was content and the soil under his nails seemed natural and good.

But the farmers grew envious of Floren. For though he was no farmer, his plants were growing higher, his corn hardier, his grain fuller than theirs. Though his father and his father's father had been wandering minstrels, he was proving to be a better man of the soil than those who had lived all their lives with the soil of Plaisant under their feet. They began to mutter among themselves.

"He does not sing a mere song," one farmer said. "He sings hymns to the devil."

"He does not sing mere hymns to the devil," said another. "He sings an incantation for his crops."

"He does not sing a mere incantation for his own crops," said a third. "He calls out curses on our crops as well."

And so it grew, this seed of envy that the neighboring farmers planted. And by the following spring it was in full flower in their hearts. All they could think of was Floren's luck, for as he flourished so they seemed to decline. And when their early plantings died, flooded out by unusual rains, while Floren's field high on the mountain foot was saved, they knew where to lay the blame.

"It is *his* fault," they said, staring at the drowned crops, as if by not saying his name aloud they would not be accountable for anything that happened.

So they blamed Floren, but they could not decide what they should do.

"Perhaps we should raze his fields," said one.

"We should set his crops ablaze," said another.

"We should send our cattle to trample on his grain."

But though each of them desired revenge, they could not agree on the means. So in the end they agreed to visit the witch who lived in a cave high up in the mountains. She was an old woman who gave nothing but evil advice, and such was their mood, they wanted to hear only the worst.

It was a long climb to her home. For each man the climb seemed endless. Their backs were furrowed with sweat long before they reached the top. And though it was hard enough to climb up alone, each man feared to be left behind, so he held on to the shirt of the man in front and, in this way, doubled the agony.

The old witch woman was nearly blind, but the men made enough noise with their curses and cries to tell her they were coming. And so often did they now mix Floren's name in their loud talk, she also knew why they had come. She greeted them when they rounded the last curve, saying, "So you wish to know what to do with that cursed Singer of Seeds."

The men were hot and tired and so their marvel grew. Surely this was a mighty witch, nearly blind yet seeing with such a clear inner eye she had known they were coming and seen their purpose. They did not understand that their own lips and hearts had already betrayed them.

"We wish..." they began and then, to a man, stopped.

The old witch smiled at them, waiting. Fear and envy were common enough coins to her. She could afford to wait.

Then one man, braver than the rest, said, "We would end his song."

"Then thrust him from you," advised the witch.

Muttering amongst themselves, the farmers could come to no agreement. At last the same man spoke up again. "He would only return. He claims the mountain sings his name. He says he has sworn to the mountain that he will be with us forever."

They agreed at last. Though none had heard Floren say it, all believed it had been said. "He swore he would be with us forever," they concurred.

"Then thrust him where he cannot return," said the old woman, making a downward motion with her hand. "Seal his lips with his own mountain and then see if he can sing." She turned her back on the farmers and went into her cave. None of them dared follow.

So there was nothing the tired men could do but go back down the mountain. They grumbled all the way.

Now all the while the farmers had made their way up and then down the mountain, Floren had been at work. He had plowed and furrowed his fields. He had sown his seed. He had weeded and watered and waited for sprouts. And all the while he sang:

> *"Sunlight and moonbright*
> *And wind through the weeds.*
> *Come up and come over,*
> *Come up and come over,*
> *Come up and come over*
> *My swift-growing seeds."*

Floren's song rose over the fields, over the meadows, up and over the mountain standing jagged against the sky.

The angry farmers, angered even further by their difficult trip down the mountainside, reached their homes late at night. And though they thought it was the ending of that same long day, it had

been a season. Such is the way with magic; such is the way with madness.

In the morning when the sun rose, the men rose, too. Each by his own hearth dressed in surly silence. They met by the crossroads that led to Floren's farm.

No one spoke to any other except in growls and signs, for they had almost lost their human tongues. And if by chance a traveler had met them on the path then, he would have thought them a pack of feral men, so fierce were their faces, so wild their eyes.

They came to Floren's farm but he was up before them. It was the time of harvest and he was out with his crops at the sun's first rays. The men were amazed—was it harvest time already? Yet they had left right after planting. They thought the hasty season was magic of Floren's making, though in fact it was they who had climbed throughout the whole growing season, and what they had grown now lay rotted in their hearts.

The farmers lifted their faces to the late summer sun, shrouded in clouds. They sniffed the air. The sounds of Floren's song drifted to them.

"Come up and come over," he sang. "Come up and come over."

The music hurt their ears. One after another they cried out their distress, and the sound was a howling in the wind.

Then they ran into Floren's field, surprising him by his corn, which was full and golden and ripe. Surrounding him, they snapped at him with their teeth and tore at him with their nails. They watched as his life's blood poured out upon the rich dark soil.

Then suddenly the beast in them departed and the sun came out from behind the clouds. Horrified at what they had done, they buried Floren under the field, under the glowing corn. They sealed his lips with the dirt of his own mountain and left, no man daring to look at his neighbor.

69

The next morning when the sun rose, it was pale and thin like a worn copper penny. Every farmer in Plaisant rose, too, hurrying to his own field. But the growing time was over, and what little had sprung up in their fields was weedy and scant. Only Floren's field, at the mountain's foot, was full of ripened corn.

As each man looked across his fields, a wind came sighing down the mountainside. It blew a song across Floren's cornfield as if on a giant reed pipe. The song was wordless, but each farmer in his field recognized it at once. Floren's corn sang in a thousand voices, as clear as doom:

> *"Sunlight and moonbright*
> *And wind through the weeds.*
> *Come up and come over,*
> *Come up and come over,*
> *Come up and come over*
> *My swift-growing seeds."*

It sang on and on that year and every year for the rest of their lives.

Every season from that time on, the corn grew without planting in Floren's field, and every season it sang his song. The wind whistled his song across the valley of Plaisant. And though passersby thought it a pleasant, cheerful song, the farmers heard a different tune. Floren was indeed with them forever.

Sometimes I write a poem for no reason other than to challenge myself. This was such a task. I looked at the poems I had already written for this collection and realized that all the rhymed poems were funny, the serious poems unrhymed. That bothered me, because it was not a statement I wanted to make, even subtly. Some of my favorite poets—John Donne, William Butler Yeats, David McCord, Anthony Hecht—wrote serious rhymed poetry. So I set myself down at the keyboard and drafted this. Then the hard work began. Revising the poem. Seven versions later it was done. Or as done as a poem ever gets. As John Ciardi once said, "A poem is never finished, it's abandoned."

In the Silvered Night

In the silent silvered night,
None but long-eared owls take flight
Above the graveyard, as if driven
To display. Below, the shriven
Souls of dead lie silent deep,
The owls do not disturb their sleep.
But rising up from shallower graves
Come those whom no one ever saves.
Snaking up like smoke, like wire,
Like paper twists uncurled in fire,
Like wraiths of fog, rise all unmourned,
The long-forgotten, unadorned,
Whose lives were bleak and black and maimed.
We see these souls and them have named:
Specters, apparitions, ghosts,
Elect of all the deadly hosts.
They do not live, they cannot die;

But somewhere in between they lie
Uncomforted in their old earth,
Which brings about a second birth.
Their anguish overcomes each death;
Their anger fills each haunt with breath.
Until we give them proper names,
Until we shrive their poor remains,
Their souls will not take honored flight
And they will roil the silvered night.

I wanted to write a dog or cat ghost story for this book but didn't know where to start, till I read Ghosts and Apparitions *by W. H. Salter. "Given poor light and a fit of nerves," he wrote, "how easy does a bush become a bear." I wanted more than that for this little tale, so I drew upon some real-life things and the story came alive for me.*

Mandy really was my dog—a big, slobbery black Labrador. We got her from a veterinarian when I was thirteen; the first dog I ever owned. When I went off to college, the member of my family I missed most was Mandy. I used to send long PSs just for her in my letters home. When I was a senior she developed a heart condition that had to be treated with a before-dinner drink every night. My father told me she adored it, in the same letter he told me that she had died quietly one evening under the weeping willow in our backyard. This story is a kind of memorial to her.

Mandy

I hated camp. I need to say that right up front. All that group singing and macramé, birch-bark constructions and skinny-dipping in the cold lake. To make things worse, the camp library consisted of a billion copies of the Fear Street books, three editions of *Johnny Tremain,* and every novel Robert Louis Stevenson ever wrote, but nothing else.

I hated camp. I was only there because Mom and Dad needed the summer to sort things out, a phrase I suspected meant they might get divorced. And me not there to explain to them in words of one syllable why they shouldn't do it: Those words were *love* and *me.*

I hated camp. I missed my dog, Mandy, awfully. We hadn't been separated for more than a single night since five years ago when we had gotten her from the vet because her owners didn't want her anymore. Mandy was a big, sloppy, slobbery, loving black Labrador who knew we were hers from the moment she saw us. Mom saw her first and said, "That one." Even at seven, I figured out that Mandy was supposed to be a kind of substitute for the three babies Mom had lost in a row, in the fourth month of each pregnancy. But Mandy was never Mom's dog. She was mine from the beginning.

I hated camp. Camp meant doing things together all day long, and I am a loner by nature. I like to read a lot. The only physical thing I like to do is go out on the beach with Mandy. She's a water dog and I'm a beach kid, Dad says. And that's what makes us such good friends.

Truth is—most of all I hated camp because I was homesick. And Mom and Dad sick. And especially Mandy sick. Of course I didn't let myself cry, because then the other kids would have been merciless, teasing me until I threw up like Carl Switzer did behind the birch tree by the crafts cabin. Or been forced to spend the night in the nurse's station like Bruce Carville, sobbing so hard the nurse got no sleep till well after midnight. Of course Carl and Bruce had the excuse of being two years younger than me.

I didn't want teasing on top of everything else, so I kept it in— the anger and the hurt and the loneliness and the homesickness. And when it hurt the most—at night in our cabin, with all the light breathy sounds of the other boys settling down into sleep, and our counselor Jim snoring loudly like some sort of engine—I found myself with an ache in my side and chest from holding things in so tightly.

I was miserable.

The third night of camp, I waited until everyone was really sound asleep. Then I got up and pulled my pants on over my pajama bottoms and a sweater over the top, because New Hampshire nights are cold, even in the summer. Then I went out.

This being summer, it was still pretty light, a kind of glistening in the air. The trees by the cabin were black, but the sky and the lake glowed. A half-moon was reflected in the water, and the stars blinked on and off like a billion distant fireflies.

As I made my way down the path toward the lake, something scrabbled away into the underbrush. Ordinarily I would have been scared. After all, not only are there are coons and squirrels and rabbits and skunks up in New Hampshire, there are also big cats, coyotes, and bears. But I sensed that whatever was in the bushes was more scared of me than I was of it. So I ignored the sound and continued on down the path.

I walked out to the end of the wooden dock, where the camp's diving lessons are held, and sat down, letting my bare feet dangle way above the water. A small breeze pulled ripples along the lake, making the moon's reflection wrinkle.

I thought about home. I thought about Mom and Dad and Mandy. I shivered with the cold, and with something more than that—with a kind of longing.

And then I heard—or rather I felt—something stepping onto the wooden dock.

When I turned to look, there was some large animal at the far end, a kind of large grey shadow. It was too big for a raccoon but not big enough for a bear. Slowly it came toward me.

Coyote?

Wolf?

I thought briefly about leaping into the water to escape it. The lake water would be cold and dark. It was deep at this end. I was wearing heavy clothes. I could easily drown.

I thought just as briefly about screaming. That would wake up all the campers and counselors in my cabin and probably all the others. If they came running out, they would scare off the wolf or coyote thing. It would probably head right into the bushes, and then no one would believe me. The aftermath of that was too awful to contemplate.

Which left me with no choice. None at all.

And then the silvery animal *whuffled.*

Whuffled! Which is a kind of sneeze deep in the throat.

It was a sound I knew well. My dog, Mandy, made such a sound when she was about to give me one of her slobbery kisses.

Not a wolf then. Not a coyote.

I stood carefully and held out my hand. "Nice doggy," I said. "I won't hurt you." I hoped the dog could say the same for me.

It came over and smelled my hand, giving it a good long lick.

The dog was the size and shape of a Labrador, but instead of black or gold, it was a kind of silver grey, which is not a Lab color at all. Its coat seemed to glow in the moonlight, and I could see the separate rough hairs on the back of its head—like silver needles, only much softer. Its silver grey tail wagged back and forth. I patted its nose, and it sat down at once, lifting a great paw up for me to shake. That was Mandy's one trick.

I shook the dog's paw solemnly. "Pleased to meet you," I said.

In answer, the dog *whuffled* again.

Then as if we had reached agreement, we sat down at the end of the dock and snuggled close—my arm over its back, its paw in my lap—and watched the moon make its double way across sky and water through the dark till dawn.

I must have dozed off before it was actually sunrise. When I woke, I was curled up, all alone on the end of the dock. But oddly, I was no longer homesick. And while I didn't suddenly *love* camp, it did suddenly seem bearable.

All that day the counselors commented on how much I finally

seemed to be fitting in. Jim said, "You've got it now, kid." The swim counselor, Mark, called me "a regular little sunfish." And after I managed to make a macramé dog collar in the crafts tent, it was hung up on the camp bulletin board as an example of good work.

And so a whole week went by, which meant seven nights as well. Each night, after the rest of the boys were asleep and Jim was deep into his engine snoring, I sneaked out of the bunk and went down to the dock to spend the dark hours with the silver dog I called Argent, which means "silver."

It wasn't an easy thing to do. The third night I scared up a raccoon. The fifth night I had to make a long and scary detour so as not to frighten a skunk. But I never hesitated, knowing that Argent would be waiting.

We didn't just stay on the dock the whole time. One night we took a long walk on the winding path that goes around the lake. Argent trembled with excitement whenever she heard some small animal in the brush, but she never left my side. And one night we made our way up to the head counselor's cottage, looking through the window as he watched the eleven o'clock news on a small, flickering black-and-white television. Argent leaned against my left leg and made a soft rumbling sound, which would have been a purr if she'd been a cat instead of a big dog. But we always ended up back on the dock, where I would fall asleep with my face in her fur, which smelled a little of lemon and a lot of dog. I never worried about being out in the dark, for I knew she would protect me all night long.

Except for my beach walks with Mandy, I don't think I've ever been happier. Which is odd, considering I was at a place I didn't

want to be, my parents were making a decision that would affect me forever, and my own real dog was far away.

But there was something wonderfully solid and comforting about Argent. Something almost magical about the way we could walk all around the camp at night with no one ever finding us out.

And then the seventh day, the week's end, as we sat close together on the end of the dock, Argent suddenly stood up. She licked my face slowly, as if her tongue was trying to memorize my features: forehead, nose, right cheek, chin, and back again. She shook herself all over and whuffled once.

Then, without any warning, she leaped into the lake.

I had often seen Mandy jump into the water that way—without fear or hesitation—after a thrown stick. But this was the middle of the night, and there was nothing for Argent to be fetching. The sound she made hitting the water was as loud as a gunshot, and spray splattered my bare feet.

"Argent!" I shouted, afraid my voice was loud enough to wake everyone in camp.

She ignored me, swimming farther and farther out into the darkness. All I could see was her silver head, like a small beacon of light above the water, getting smaller and smaller.

I ran back to the shore and shoved one of the camp rowboats into the water, with more strength than I knew I had. Disregarding my soaked pants, I clambered in, and slipping the oars into the oarlocks, I began to row. I was not very good at it, and I kept beating the oars on the top of the water instead of slicing the blades swiftly and cleanly through. And I couldn't seem to get the boat to go in a straight line at all. But at last I rowed out to the place where I had last seen Argent's silvery head, and looked around.

She was gone.

I stood up so I could see farther, and the boat rocked so hard, the oars slipped out of the oarlocks. I reached desperately over the side for one, and the entire boat overturned, spilling me into the cold, dark lake.

I plunged down deep and kicked desperately to go up. My heavy clothes hindered my rise, and I fought to rip off my sweater. The hard part was getting the soaking thing over my head. But at last I was free of it. With one final kick I broke the surface of the water and took in a great gulp of air.

"Help!" I began to scream. "Help!"

I managed to swim over to the rowboat and hold on to the side, but I was shivering unceasingly with the cold.

"Help!" I screamed again.

A light went on in one cabin. Then another. There were suddenly a hundred small bobbing lights, like antic fireflies, as people rushed about outside.

"In the water!" I screamed. "I'm in the water."

And then, before anyone could actually get a boat pushed off from shore, I felt something shove up under my arm.

I looked at the shiny silver snout.

"Argent!" I cried. "You've come back."

She pushed me toward shore, toward the one rowboat that was finally heading for me.

Then hands reached down and hauled me into the boat, and I lay wheezing on the bottom.

Someone shouted, "We've got him!"

Someone else—I think it was Jim—said, "Jeez, Willy, what were you doing out in a boat after midnight?"

And I took a deep breath and said, "The dog..."

"What dog?" Jim asked.

I raised myself up and stared out across the water. I could see

Argent's silver head going back across the lake, disappearing into the darkness. I didn't have the strength to point at her, or to call after her.

I knew even then she would never be back.

I was sent home the next day. My counselor, Jim, went with me. I think the camp was glad to let me go. Afraid of lawsuits, most likely. I didn't care. Without Argent there, I certainly didn't want to stay.

Mom and Dad met me at the door, and Mom enveloped me in a huge hug. Dad shook Jim's hand and made him tell the story of my rescue three times, asking questions at every change in it.

"There was no dog, sir," Jim explained again. "They aren't allowed at the camp."

At the mention of the dog, I was suddenly aware of the one member of the family who wasn't there.

"Where's Mandy?" I asked. "Where is she?"

Mom looked at Dad, and then sighed. "Tell him," she said in a voice that sounded like a death sentence.

Dad took me by the hand and made me sit down. "Willy, last week Mandy got sick. Very sick. It was as if she was fading in front of our eyes. She didn't even have the energy to go for a walk on the beach. The vet said it was her heart and the only thing we could do was to give her a little bit of alcohol before bedtime. A lemon cordial. To stimulate her heart."

"You mean like a drink?" I asked.

"A doggy cocktail," Mom said.

"Did she like it?"

"She was a regular party girl!" Dad said, smiling a little.

"For a bit," Mom said, taking up the burden of the story, "she seemed to perk up. I took her for gentle walks on the shore."

81

"Didn't want either of my girls overdoing it," Dad said, looking fondly at Mom. "Not in their conditions."

I think my jaw dropped.

"Past the fifth month, and all is well," Mom said to me, patting her belly. "We sent you to camp so I could take it very easy at this particular time."

"All is well, that is, except for Mandy," Dad added.

"What happened?"

"Last night I went out to call her in for her cocktail, and she didn't come. I called and called and finally went out and found her under the willow."

"Her favorite place," I said.

He nodded. "I gave her her lemon cordial, and for a little while she rallied, sitting up and shoving her nose under my arm."

He was silent for a moment, and I didn't dare ask what happened next. I wanted to know . . . but at the same time, I didn't.

"And then she got this faraway look in her eyes, as if she were no longer there," Dad said. "She put her head on my arm and gave that funny little sound."

"The whuffling."

"Yes, Willy, the whuffling. And then she—was gone."

He didn't say she had died, but that she was gone, which was unlike my father.

Mom came over and sat down by me, and put her arm around my shoulder. "I wish you had been here, Willy. To say good-bye."

I thought about that brave, ghostly silver head held high over the dark water, going away into the darkness. "I couldn't come to her, Mom, so she came to me."

They both looked at me oddly, and Jim was suddenly busy tugging at a loose button on his shirt. But I smiled.

"She came a long way, a moonlit dog, silvered like a ghost. She came so we could say our good-byes."

Jim pulled the button off and slipped it into his pocket. Dad stared down at his shoes. But Mom looked right into my eyes.

"Mandy was that kind of a dog," she said. And kissed me on the forehead, nose, and chin.

Sitting by the big, curved window in the living room of our house in Scotland, a cup of tea beside me, I gazed out at the garden, at the wind puzzling through the wisteria. I was thinking about this book and wondering who I would haunt if I had the chance. This poem was my answer.

Haunt

When I am gone,
Who will I haunt?
The second-grade teacher
Who screamed at me
For letting a plant die
Over the Christmas break?
The girl who stole
My junior high boyfriend
Because she could dance the frug
And I could not?
The boy in high school
With the big ears
Who stood by his locker
And made nasty sounds
When I walked past?
Or the one in college
Who said he loved me
But married someone else?

I have let them go long since;
Even their names have disappeared
Like stones in water,

Where the ripples extend outward
For a little while and then,
With a shimmer, are gone.
Life is too short for haunting,
Memories too long to waste.
I do not envy ghosts
Their righteous anger,
Their unhappy recall.
Instead, after death
I will be with those I love,
In a gentler way,
Coming to them in a swirl of apple blossom,
On the wings of chocolate,
In the twist of steam from a cup of tea
Set out on the countertop to cool.

Bruce Coville and I were working together on a novel called Armageddon Summer. *We had been going at the revisions for three solid days and needed a break. So we took a walk along the Connecticut River near my house, still arguing over how the book was going. On our way back, we passed a de-sanctified church that had been the living quarters of one Hatfield family for the past thirteen years. The man of the house was painting the outside, and we stopped to talk to him. He told us there had been green ghosts in the place when he and his wife had moved in, and that a "white witch" from Turner's Falls had gotten rid of them, though his dog had howled and the hair on the back of the man's hands had stood up during the exorcism. "Of course," he said, "I don't believe in this sort of stuff—ghosts and UFOs. But there they were." Bruce and I argued over which one of us could use the details in a story. As it was my home town and I had a ghost collection coming up, I declared the story was mine. (But don't be surprised if Bruce writes one, too!)*

Green Ghosts

The day we moved into our new house, I saw the green ghosts, only at first, I didn't know what they were.

"Bats," I said to my stepmom, who was unpacking boxes downstairs in the finished basement that was to be our home. Our home, that is, until Dad could rebuild the first floor as a living room and kitchen.

"Of course bats," my stepmom said. "Bats in the belfry." She lifted her chin toward the upstairs.

And that made sense because our new house used to be a Lutheran church before it had been *de-sanctified*, which is a word that took me a whole day of fifth grade to learn. It means it was "dechurched." Made unholy and ready to be lived in instead of prayed in.

"Green bats," I added. "With long green tails."

My stepmom shook her head. "Bats aren't green," she said.

"And they don't have long tails," I agreed.

So she grabbed Joey out of his playpen, and with our golden Lab, Ruff, trotting at her heels, she went up with me to investigate.

There was a strange slant of afternoon light coming through the stained-glass windows, filtering down in dusty rays. The old pews, still lined up in straight rows like an army at attention, seemed to be waiting for a congregation. For almost a minute there was no movement, no sound beyond our own ragged breathing.

Then Ruff sat down, raised his head, looked wild-eyed at the ceiling, and began to howl. It was an unearthly sound that I had never heard him make before.

"Shut up!" I cautioned, but he kept on howling.

As if answering Ruff's awful sound, the green things came down from the rafters, flying slow ellipses, their phosphorescent tails lingering behind them. *Ellipses* and *phosphorescent* were vocabulary words from sixth grade. I was glad to have them.

"Birdie!" said Joey. "Mine!" He reached a hand out toward the lowest one.

My stepmom stared for a long moment then, clutching Joey to her shoulder, she gave a huge scream before running out of the front door and down the stairs.

Still howling, Ruff followed her, his tail safely tucked between his legs.

I didn't go at once. I wanted to be sure I could describe to Dad what the green things were. I know how to do that because we go bird-watching together, and remembering what flying things look like is a big part of what bird-watching's all about.

The green things were about three feet long and sort of diaph-anous, which was a spelling word we had last week. It means you could see through them. The green was more like the color of bubbles in the sea. But when one of the things got up close to me, I saw it had a human face—an old woman's face, to be exact. An *angry* old woman. That's when I bolted out of there. I already had more than enough for a description.

I didn't exactly scream like my stepmom, but I wasn't exactly quiet either.

Dad met me at the bottom step.

"Mary Brigid," he said, which is what he calls me when he's mad, "what in blazes are you and Kim carrying on for? All of Harford will hear you."

"Green bats," my stepmom said from behind him, her voice going up and down the scale and not in any recognizable order.

"Pretty," said Joey.

"Ghosts," I said.

Ruff's howl had diminished—which was another of our fifth-grade spelling words—to a moan.

"Guess that church was not so de-sanctified after all," I added.

"Bless me," said Dad, and went up for a look himself because he's not the kind of person to take anyone else's word on matters of faith. Or flying things.

When he came down the stairs again, he was white faced, and his jaw had dropped so far down, it was nearly dislocated. A fourth-grade word but useful.

"We need a priest," he said, which was odd since he hadn't been to mass in ages. Not since he and my mother got divorced.

Which is how we got Father Cogan. Who got Bishop Terrigan. Who got Monseigneur Karski. Who got us the white witch from Turner's Falls. Who came the next day.

89

The white witch wasn't at all what I expected. In the first place, he was a man, tall and cadaverous—a spelling word from last year that means really thin to the point of looking like a skeleton. His cheekbones could have almost cut a loaf of bread. He had long bony fingers. In the second place, he was covered with black hair. Not just on his head but on his cheeks and chin, and the backs of his hands as well. In the third place, he had a rather high voice, squeaky almost. In the fourth, he was carrying a big black duffel bag with PROPERTY OF UMASS ATHLETICS on the side.

"Green ghosts," he said, "are my speciality."

My stepmom was still at the Bide-a-wee Motel, where we'd spent the night. She had wanted to keep me there, as well. But I had insisted on coming back to the church with Dad. And when the white witch—whose name was John Simeon—said that about green ghosts, I had to ask.

"Seen many?"

"All the time," he said in his squeaky voice, which reminded me of a slowly opening door in a scary movie. "Don't you worry, little lady."

"I'm not worried," I said. "I was just curious, that's all."

He and my father smiled over my head, that grown-up smile that means they understand more than they are telling, and it's nothing a kid could understand anyway. I hate that smile. I will never use it when I grow up.

Then the witch added, "Green ghosts are the souls of departed parishioners who are still hanging around a church after it has been de-sanctified. They just need to be told it's time to go."

Easy enough, I thought, and turned, pointing at the door. In the loudest voice I could muster, I shouted, "Go home, ghosts!"

"It's not quite that simple," said John Simeon. "There are rules."

"Rules?" I asked. "Like in spelling?"

"She's the regional spelling champ," said my dad, as if that explained my question. "You may have seen her on TV."

"Just like in spelling," agreed John Simeon. "Only you won't see it televised."

"Noncorporeal?" I asked. Seventh-grade word.

"Nonpublishable," he replied. "Needs to be kept secret."

"Cool," I said. "I'm good at secrets."

"Mary Brigid!" Dad warned. If his voice could have lifted me out of there, I'd have been gone that moment. "The first rule is: No kids allowed."

"That's not one of the rules, I bet . . ." I began, glancing at John Simeon for confirmation.

But Dad didn't wait. "Downstairs! Now!" He took me by the shoulder and marched me to the door that led to the basement.

I went willingly, with only the slightest show of reluctance—a fourth-grade word that can include foot dragging and a long face. But I wasn't totally upset. After all, I had discovered a small, secret way from my bedroom up to the choir loft, which Dad didn't know about. The only problem was, the third and seventh steps squeaked worse than the white witch's voice, so I was careful not to step on either one.

Leaning against the loft railings, I could both see and hear John Simeon at work, though his squeaky voice didn't carry words so much as emotions up to me. As I watched, he reached into the black duffel and took out thirteen white candles, the fat kind they sell at Easter. With Dad's help, he set them out on the steps in a line in front of the pulpit. He went back to the duffel and pulled out branches, which he placed around the candles in a complicated

91

pattern. Then he sprinkled something like salt over the top of the whole thing and lit the candles one at a time with a small lighter. The smoke from the candles spiraled up, looking a bit like ghost tails.

The green ghosts had hung back at first, but when John Simeon had gotten to the salt thing, they started to dive-bomb him and Dad, like some passionate kamikaze pilots from World War II. (Seventh-grade history, first semester.) All but one, a little green ghost—the only one who seemed to notice me. It made a silent strafing run along the choir-loft bannister, right toward my head. At the last minute, as silent as the ghost, I ducked and covered my head with my arms. I didn't want to call attention to myself, but I didn't want to get battered, either. The ghostlet—because it seemed to be a very small ghost—got confused at my ducking down, and continued straight into the choir-loft wall, knocking itself silly and flopping down onto the floor, next to me.

"Noncorporeal, my foot!" I whispered, reaching out a hand to it. It felt a bit like Jell-O, only Jell-O that I could put my finger right through. My finger got all prickly where it went in, the way you feel when an appendage—sixth-grade word, which the boys giggled at but I never thought particularly funny—goes to sleep.

Just then John Simeon began to chant, and his voice changed from a squeak to a throbbing boom. It was the chant that did it, and the chant was in some other language, Latin maybe. Or Hebrew. Or even Greek. It simply rolled out of his mouth and became almost palpable—a vocabulary word from last week that means "touched or felt or readily perceived." Like a net, the palpable chant gathered in those green ghosts, and they flopped about in it like phosphorescent fish at the side of a trawler.

In a moment, they were all gathered in.

All—except for the little ghost, still knocked out, next to my hand.

I could have called down then and said, "Hey, Mr. White Witch, there's one more ghost fish to be caught up here." But then my dad would have known I'd disobeyed him.

And even more, the little ghost—who was now staring up at me, young and scared and not at all ready to be sent away from the only home it could remember—would be gone.

So I didn't say a word. This is what is known in church as a sin of omission. Meaning "leaving out." I like the fact that the word *mission* is at the end of it!

I put my finger up to my lips and nodded meaningfully at the little green ghost.

Eyes wide, the little ghost understood and nodded back.

I raised myself a little above the choir-loft bannister and watched as John Simeon raised his hands up like a priest giving a blessing. His voice boomed out something more in Latin. (Or Hebrew. Or even Greek.) Then he bent over and blew out the thirteen candles, one by one by one.

Like candles going out, the ghosts caught in the net guttered out. One minute there, the next minute gone.

"That's done then," John Simeon said in his squeaky voice.

"The hairs on the back of my neck were sticking straight out when you began to chant," my Dad said.

"That's how you know it's working," said John Simeon. "I watch the back of my hands. See..." They both looked down at his hairy hands.

While they were occupied with that, I gathered up the little green ghost and headed back down the stairs, being sure not to step on the seventh or third step. The ghost nestled in my arms, its long tail draping over my fingers. I could feel the prickles starting along the whole of my hand, wherever the ghost touched. It felt warm and raspy, like a cat's licking tongue. There was a strange, grateful look on the ghost's phosphorescent face. A young face, not much older, I would guess, than my half brother.

I had no idea what I was going to say to Mom or Dad or Kim. But I knew what I was going to tell Joey. "Mine!"

I clutched the little green ghost to me and settled down in my favorite reading chair, a spelling book to hand.

"Frugal," I read aloud to the ghost. "It means 'to save.' But not— I think—this kind." I continued to read until the little ghost, tired out from its day, fell asleep in my arms.

My editor phoned after I had turned in the manuscript of Here There Be Ghosts. *"You need a really scary story," he said. I wasn't sure whether I could do really scary. Most readers, if asked, would define really scary as something with buckets of blood and major splattering. Hollywood has a lot to answer for. But my ghost writing is hardly that. It is about souls in trouble; it is about which incidents in our lives really haunt us. Still, I always try to give my editor what he wants. So I sent this short short story to him, thinking as I did so that I had failed to do his bidding. He phoned to say that he thought this tale was "the most frightening ghost story imaginable."*

Souls

When the boy was small and playing in the kitchen, a fly lit on his arm. He picked the fly up between his thumb and forefinger and showed it to his grandmother, who was making küchen.

"Grossmutter," he asked, "what is this?"

"Nothing," she said, taking the fly from him and popping it between her fingers. "It is only a fly. There. Gone."

"Did it hurt the fly?"

"It did not hurt."

"Will it go to heaven?"

"Flies do not go to heaven."

"Will it be a ghost?"

"Flies have no souls, and so they have no ghosts."

"That is good." He smiled up at his grandmother with the sweetest smile and went outside to play.

———

When he was a little older, he found a worm in the garden. He picked it up between his thumb and forefinger. He took it to his grandfather, who was cutting grass with a long scythe.

"Grosspapa," he asked, "what is this?"

"Nothing," the old man said, taking the worm from him and squeezing it between his fingers. "Only a worm. There. It bothers you no more."

"Did it hurt the worm?"

"Worms feel no pain."

"Will the worm go to heaven?"

"Worms do not go to heaven. Only people go to heaven."

"Will it be a ghost?"

"Worms and other creepers have no souls, and so they have no ghosts."

"That is good," the boy said. He smiled up at his grandfather and went back to digging in the soil.

When he was older still, the boy saw a farmer carrying a litter of kittens in a canvas bag.

"What are you doing?" asked the boy.

"I am going to drown them," said the farmer. "There are already too many kittens in the world, and so I make sure there are a few less."

"Will it hurt them?"

"A moment, no more."

"Will they go to heaven?"

"Only people go to heaven. Not animals."

"So there will be no ghosts to haunt us?"

"Animals have no souls, so they have no ghosts to haunt us."

"That is good," said the boy. "May I do it for you?"

"If you wish," said the farmer.

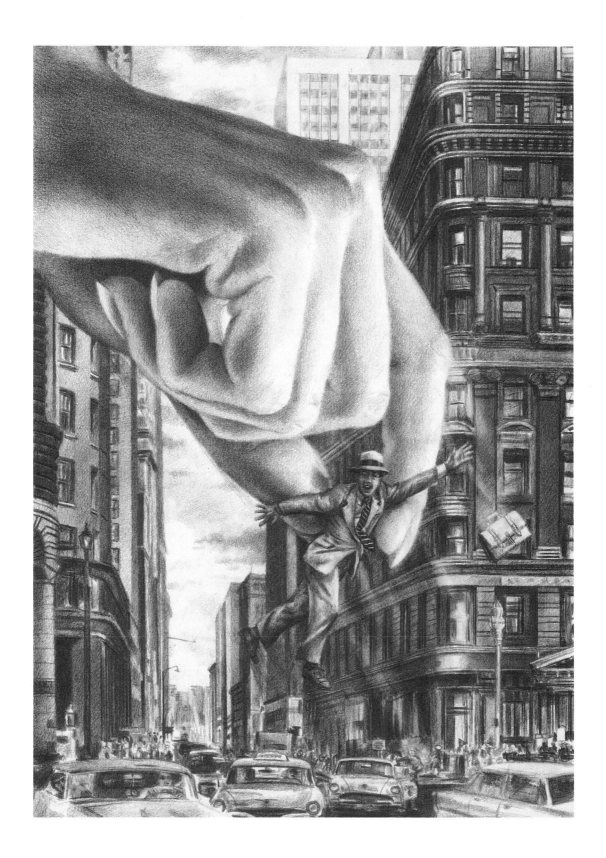

The boy took the bag from the farmer and drowned the kittens, one at a time. He did it with exquisite care, so they should not feel any pain.

When he was yet still older, the boy shot a dog, and then a deer, and then a bear. He knew they were not going to go to heaven. He knew they had no souls.

"If they have no souls," he told himself, "they will have no ghosts to haunt me."

And they did not.

Eventually the boy became a man.

He killed black people and Gypsies and crippled people and Jews.

"Do you not worry their ghosts will haunt you?" someone asked him. "Are you not afraid?"

"They are only animals," he said. "And animals have no souls. So—no, I am not worried about being haunted by them."

And he was not.

But in the middle of his life, a gigantic hand came out of the sky and plucked him up between a massive thumb and forefinger.

"Put me down!" he screamed. "Let me go."

But the hand did not put him down. The great fingers closed upon him.

"You cannot treat me like this," he cried. "I am a man. Let me go, or I shall haunt you forever."

"A man? I do not think so. In all your life, you have never shown that you have a soul," said a great voice that was both gentle as water and as hard. "So why should I be afraid of your ghost?"

The great fingers squeezed shut.

Over twenty years ago I was working on my master's degree at the University of Massachusetts. I took a course on Victorian and Edwardian children's literature at Smith College. (All five colleges in the Pioneer Valley, where I live, let students mix and match their courses.) One of the texts I got to reread was George MacDonald's wonderful novel The Princess and the Goblin. *In the book there is a strong and mystical mother figure, living in a tower, who aids the princess with a golden rope. I was also working on a paper called "America's Cinderella" for a folklore course. The two seemed to combine in this story, which I wrote at the same time. The majestic mother-sister in this story is both an apparition (a kind of ghost) and a symbolic figure. The tale was first published in a collection of mine called* The Moon Ribbon and Other Tales.*

The Moon Ribbon

There was once a plain but good-hearted girl named Sylva whose sole possession was a ribbon her mother had left her. It was a strange ribbon, the color of moonlight, for it had been woven from the grey hairs of her mother and her mother's mother and her mother's mother's mother before her.

Sylva lived with her widowed father in a great house by the forest's edge. Once the great house had belonged to her mother, but when she died, it became Sylva's father's house to do with as he willed. And what he willed was to live simply and happily with his daughter without thinking of the day to come.

But one day, when there was little enough to live on, and only the great house to recommend him, Sylva's father married again, a beautiful widow who had two beautiful daughters of her own.

It was a disastrous choice, for no sooner were they wed when it

99

was apparent the woman was mean in spirit and meaner in tongue. She dismissed most of the servants and gave their chores over to Sylva, who followed her orders without complaint. For simply living in her mother's house with her loving father seemed enough for the girl.

After a bit, however, the old man died in order to have some peace, and the house passed on to the stepmother. Scarcely two days had gone by, or maybe three, when the stepmother left off mourning the old man and turned on Sylva. She dismissed the last of the servants without their pay.

"Girl," she called out, for she never used Sylva's name, "you will sleep in the kitchen and do the charring." And from that time on it was so.

Sylva swept the floor and washed and mended the family's clothing. She sowed and hoed and tended the fields. She ground the wheat and kneaded the bread, and she waited on the others as though she were a servant. But she did not complain.

Yet late at night, when the stepmother and her own two daughters were asleep, Sylva would weep bitterly into her pillow, which was nothing more than an old broom laid in front of the hearth.

One day, when she was cleaning out an old desk, Sylva came upon a hidden drawer she had never seen before. Trembling, she opened the drawer. It was empty except for a silver ribbon with a label attached to it. *For Sylva* read the card. *The Moon Ribbon of Her Mother's Hair.* She took it out and stared at it. And all that she had lost was borne in upon her. She felt the tears start in her eyes, and so as not to cry she took the tag off and began to stroke the ribbon with her hand. It was rough and smooth at once and shone like the rays of the moon.

At that moment her stepsisters came into the room.

"What is that?" asked one. "Is it nice? It is mine."

101

"I want it. I saw it first," cried the other.

The noise brought the stepmother to them. "Show it to me," she said.

Obediently, Sylva came over and held the ribbon out to her. But when the stepmother picked it up, it looked like no more than strands of grey hair woven together unevenly. It was prickly to the touch.

"Disgusting," said the stepmother dropping it back into Sylva's hand. "Throw it out at once."

"Burn it," cried one stepsister.

"Bury it," cried the other.

"Oh, please. It was my mother's. She left it for me. Please let me keep it," begged Sylva.

The stepmother looked again at the grey strand. "Very well," she said with a grim smile. "It suits you." And she strode out of the room, her daughters behind her.

Now that she had the silver ribbon, Sylva thought her life would be better. But instead it became worse. As if to punish her for speaking out for the ribbon, her sisters were at her to wait on them both day and night. And whereas before she had to sleep by the hearth, she now had to sleep outside with the animals. Yet she did not complain or run away, for she was tied by her memories to her mother's house.

One night, when the frost was on the grass turning each blade into a silver spear, Sylva threw herself to the ground in tears. And the silver ribbon, which she had tied loosely about her hair, slipped off and lay on the ground before her. She had never seen it in the moonlight. It glittered and shone and seemed to ripple.

Sylva bent over to touch it and her tears fell upon it. Suddenly the ribbon began to grow and change, and as it changed, the air was filled with a woman's soft voice speaking these words:

"Silver ribbon, silver hair,
Carry Sylva with great care,
Bring my daughter home."

And there at Sylva's feet was a silver river that glittered and shone and rippled in the moonlight.

There was neither boat nor bridge, but Sylva did not care. She thought the river would wash away her sorrows, and without a single word, she threw herself in.

But she did not sink. Instead she floated like a swan and the river bore her on, on past houses and hills, past high places and low. And strange to say, she was not wet at all.

At last she was carried around a deep bend in the river and deposited gently on a grassy slope that came right down to the water's edge. Sylva scrambled up onto the bank and looked about. There was a great meadow of grass so green and still, it might have been painted on. At the meadow's rim, near a dark forest, sat a house that was like and yet not like the one in which Sylva lived.

Surely someone will be there who can tell me where I am and why I have been brought here, she thought. So she made her way across the meadow, and only where she stepped down did the grass move. When she moved beyond, the grass sprang back and was the same as before. And though she passed larkspur and meadowsweet, clover and rye, they did not seem like real flowers, for they had no smell at all.

Am I dreaming? she wondered, *or am I dead?* But she did not say it out loud, for she was afraid to speak into the silence.

Sylva walked up to the house and hesitated at the door. She feared to knock and yet feared equally not to. As she was deciding, the door opened of itself and she walked in.

She found herself in a large, long, dark hall with a single crystal door at the end that emitted a strange glow the color of moonlight. As she walked down the hall, her shoes made no clatter on the polished wood floor. And when she reached the door, she tried to peer through into the room beyond, but the crystal panes merely gave back her own reflection twelve times.

Sylva reached for the doorknob and pulled sharply. The glowing crystal knob came off in her hand. She would have wept then, but anger stayed her; she beat her fist against the door and it suddenly gave way.

Inside was a small room lit only by a fireplace and a round, white globe that hung from the ceiling like a pale, wan moon. Before the fireplace stood a tall woman dressed all in white. Her silver white hair was unbound and cascaded to her knees. Around her neck was a silver ribbon.

"Welcome, my daughter," she said.

"Are you my mother?" asked Sylva wonderingly, for what little she remembered of her mother, she remembered no one as grand as this.

"I am if you make me so," came the reply.

"And how do I do that?" asked Sylva.

"Give me your hand."

As the woman spoke, she seemed to move away, yet she moved not at all. Instead the floor between them moved and cracked apart. Soon they were separated by a great chasm, which was so black it seemed to have no bottom.

"I cannot reach," said Sylva.

"You must try," the woman replied.

So Sylva clutched the crystal knob to her breast and leaped, but it was too far. As she fell, she heard a woman's voice speaking from behind her and before her and all about her, warm with praise.

"Well done, my daughter. You are halfway home."

Sylva landed gently on the meadow grass, but a moment's walk from her house. In her hand she still held the knob, shrunk now to the size of a jewel. The river shimmered once before her and was gone, and where it had been was the silver ribbon, lying limp and damp in the morning frost.

The door to the house stood open. She drew a deep breath and went in.

"What is that?" cried one of the stepsisters when she saw the crystalline jewel in Sylva's hand.

"I want it," cried the other, grabbing it from her.

"I will take that," said the stepmother, snatching it from them all. She held it up to the light and examined it. "It will fetch a good price and repay me for my care of you. Where did you get it?" she asked Sylva.

Sylva tried to tell them of the ribbon and the river, the tall woman and the black crevasse. But they laughed at her and did not believe her. Yet they could not explain away the jewel. So they left her then and went off to the city to sell it. When they returned, it was late. They thrust Sylva outside to sleep and went themselves to their comfortable beds to dream of their new riches.

Sylva sat on the cold ground and thought about what had happened. She reached up and took down the ribbon from her hair. She stroked it, and it felt smooth and soft and yet hard, too. Carefully she placed it on the ground.

In the moonlight, the ribbon glittered and shone. Sylva recalled the song she had heard, so she sang it to herself:

> *"Silver ribbon, silver hair,*
>   *Carry Sylva with great care,*
>   *Bring my daughter home."*

Suddenly the ribbon began to grow and change, and there at her feet was a silver highway that glittered and glistened in the moonlight.

Without a moment's hesitation, Sylva got up and stepped out onto the road and waited for it to bring her to the magical house.

But the road did not move.

"Strange," she said to herself. "Why does it not carry me as the river did?"

Sylva stood on the road and waited a moment more, then tentatively set one foot in front of the other. As soon as she had set off on her own, the road set off, too, and they moved together past fields and forests, faster and faster, till the scenery seemed to fly by and blur into a moon-bleached rainbow of yellows, greys, and black.

The road took a great turning and then quite suddenly stopped, but Sylva did not. She scrambled up the bank where the road ended and found herself again in the meadow. At the far rim of the grass, where the forest began, was the house she had seen before.

Sylva strode purposefully through the grass, and this time the meadow was filled with the song of birds, the meadowlark and the bunting and the sweet *jug-jug-jug* of the nightingale. She could smell fresh-mown hay and the pungent pine.

The door of the house stood wide open, so Sylva went right in. The long hall was no longer dark but filled with the strange moonglow. And when she reached the crystal door at the end and gazed at her reflection twelve times in the glass, she saw her own face set with strange grey eyes and long grey hair. She put her hand up to her mouth to stop herself from crying out. But the sound came through, and the door opened of itself.

Inside was the tall woman all in white, and the globe above her was as bright as a harvest moon.

"Welcome, my sister," the woman said.

"I have no sister," said Sylva, "but the two stepsisters I left at home. And you are none of those."

"I am if you make me so."

"How do I do that?"

"Give me back my heart, which you took from me yesterday."

"I did not take your heart. I took nothing but a crystal jewel."

The woman smiled. "It was my heart."

Sylva looked stricken. "But I cannot give it back. My stepmother took it from me."

"No one can take unless you give."

"I had no choice."

"There is always a choice," the woman said.

Sylva would have cried then, but a sudden thought struck her. "Then it must have been your choice to give me your heart."

The woman smiled again, nodded gently, and held out her hand.

Sylva placed her hand in the woman's, and there glowed for a moment on the woman's breast a silvery jewel that melted and disappeared.

"Now will you give me your heart?"

"I have done that already," said Sylva, and as she said it, she knew it to be true.

The woman reached over and touched Sylva on her breast, and her heart sprang out onto the woman's hand and turned into two fiery red jewels. "Once given, twice gained," said the woman. She handed one of the jewels back to Sylva. "Only take care that you give the jewel with love."

Sylva felt the jewel, warm and glowing in her hand, and at its touch felt such comfort as she had not in many days. She closed her eyes and a smile came on her face. And when she opened her eyes again, she was standing on the meadow grass not two steps from her own door. It was morning, and by her feet lay the silver ribbon, limp and damp from the frost.

The door to her house stood open.

Sylva drew in her breath, picked up the ribbon, and went in.

"What has happened to your hair?" asked one stepsister.

"What has happened to your eyes?" asked the other.

For indeed Sylva's hair and eyes had turned as silver as the moon.

But the stepmother saw only the fiery red jewel in Sylva's hand. "Give it to me," she said, pointing to the gem.

At first Sylva held out her hand, but then quickly drew it back. "I *can* not," she said.

The stepmother's eyes became hard. "Girl, give it here."

"I *will* not," said Sylva.

The stepmother's eyes narrowed. "Then you shall tell me where you got it."

"That I shall, and gladly," said Sylva. She told them of the silver ribbon and the silver road, of the house with the crystal door. But strange to say, she left out the woman and her words.

The stepmother closed her eyes and thought. At last she said, "Let me see this wondrous silver ribbon, that I may believe what you say."

Sylva handed her the ribbon, but she was not fooled by her stepmother's tone.

The moment the silver ribbon lay prickly and limp in the stepmother's hand, she looked up triumphantly at Sylva. Her face broke into a wolfish grin. "Fool," she said, "the magic is herein. With this ribbon there are jewels for the taking." She marched out of the door and the stepsisters hurried behind her.

Sylva walked after them, but slowly, stopping in the open door.

The stepmother flung the ribbon down. In the early morning sun it glowed as if with a cold flame.

"Say the words, girl," the stepmother commanded.

From the doorway Sylva whispered:

"Silver ribbon, silver hair,
Lead the ladies with great care,
Lead them to their home."

The silver ribbon wriggled and writhed in the sunlight, and as they watched, it turned into a silver red stair that went down into the ground.

"Wait," called Sylva. "Do not go." But it was too late.

With a great shout, the stepmother gathered up her skirts and ran down the steps, her daughters fast behind her. And before Sylva could move, the ground had closed up after them and the meadow was as before.

On the grass lay the silver ribbon, limp and dull. Sylva went over and picked it up. As she did so, the jewel melted in her hand and she felt a burning in her breast. She put her hand up to it, and she felt her heart beating strongly beneath. Sylva smiled, put the silver ribbon in her pocket, and went back into her house.

After a time, Sylva's hair returned to its own color, except for seven silver strands, but her eyes never changed back. And when she was married and had a child of her own, Sylva plucked the silver strands from her own hair and wove them into the silver ribbon, which she kept in a wooden box. When Sylva's child was old enough to understand, the box with the ribbon was put into her safekeeping, and she has kept them for her own daughter to this very day.

This is the second "really scary" story I tried for my editor. It is more traditional than "Souls," though I do not know if it is scarier. Certainly the most affecting hauntings come about when the desire to talk one last time to a loved one overcomes common sense. I have peppered this story with references to my real life. Tim Banister was my daughter's first boyfriend back in high school. I borrowed the name Selan from a girl I knew in junior high. Meacham is the last name of an editor friend. And while there's always at least one girl like Maureen McNeer in high school, I know no one of that name. "Prom Ghost" took weeks of writing and rewriting to make it work, slowed down by the fact that for nearly a month I was flat on my back with a damaged sciatic nerve. The ending was changed three times. Is the story scary enough? I don't know. But if I had to go back to a prom, I would find that scary all on its own.

Prom Ghost

The night of the junior prom five years ago, Thom Selan, the football captain, and Maureen McNeer, the head cheerleader, drove off the side of the road, into the water-filled quarry north of town. A month later, divers finally brought up the car, an old Pontiac Firebird that Thom had spent months reconditioning.

Their ghosts have been wandering around the high school ever since.

The guys have seen Thom at football practice at least once a year, standing on the sidelines and yelling something at the quarterback. Only since he's a ghost, he doesn't make any sound at all, so who knows what he's saying.

And Maureen has been spotted on more than one occasion in the girls' bathroom, sneaking a cigarette, and blowing those smoke rings that were her one party trick. The shape of them lingers long after she's faded away.

I'd never run into either one. I had hated Maureen alive and even more after she was dead. So I didn't care if I ever bumped into her.

As for Thom, he was my brother, and I always thought if I got to see him, I'd probably yell: "Why did you do it? Why did you die? Why did you have to leave me?"

Because he did it on purpose. He must have. There were no skid marks at the quarry's edge. No sign that it had been an accident. He left Mom a note saying he loved her and not to wait up.

There was no note for me.

Nothing.

I couldn't forgive him that.

Mom had been crazy before the accident, unable to work, sure that people were talking about her. Lucky for us she has a trust fund or we'd probably have starved. After the accident she was inconsolable. Even five years down the line, she acted as if Thom had died just the night before.

In a way I can understand that. Thom was always her favorite. I was only an afterthought, a way of trying to save her faltering marriage. I didn't mend what couldn't be fixed, though, and Dad left even before I was born. If I've seen him ten times in seventeen years, that's a lot. He's got his own problems, and the least of them is me.

But none of that had ever mattered before because I always had Thom.

Thom was not only my big brother, he was my best friend. Five years older than me, he baby-sat me when I was little, and took me to interesting places when I got bigger—like to museums and puppet shows and, when he could drive, to things like the Harlem Globetrotters and First Night in Springfield, which is an entire day and evening of events to celebrate the new year.

111

In return I cheered at his football games and his basketball games and even for his baseball games, though the baseball team really stunk. I worshiped at the Thom altar, Maureen used to say, when she broke into our lives. Well, it's true I gave Thom unreserved love. But not unquestioning love. I questioned him all the time. His nickname for me was Little Why.

But for all my questions, the only thing we ever really disagreed about was Maureen McNeer.

"I love her, Little Why," he told me.

"She's 'tupid!" I said, our old word, the one we had used from the time we were young and weren't allowed to say bad things about people. "Really 'tupid."

"She's beautiful," he answered.

That she certainly was. She was made of moonbeams and sun motes and gossamer. Gold hair and large blue eyes and a mouth that was full and white teeth without flaws. A body that was long and toned and perfect. I had read a lot of fairy tales, and what Maureen McNeer had was *glamour*. Not movie-star glamour but the kind the old fairies commanded. The glamour that put an incandescent beauty over a toad, that turned rotten leaves into gold coins.

But she was 'tupid nonetheless. By that I didn't mean Maureen was dumb. Well, not *only* dumb. She was also tone-deaf to the universe. She saw nothing beautiful in the world that was not first reflected in her own mirror. Other people mattered to her only if they served a purpose for her. I was Thom's little sister, so she courted me at the beginning, until she was sure of him. It was so she would look wonderful in Thom's eyes. And then, when she saw me as a rival for his attention, I became the Enemy.

Once, about two months into their dating, we were playing cards—Go Fish, I think it was—and she cheated, not well but automatically and openly. When I called her on it, she laughed. She had a tinkly laugh, the kind only pretty girls seem to have.

"Of course I cheated," she said. "I couldn't let a little kid beat me, now, could I?" Of course I wasn't all that little. I was twelve.

To make it worse, Thom laughed, too. Later on he said to me, "If she had done it sneakily, Little Why, that would have been bad. But it never occurs to her to be less than open. That's what I love about her."

But the problem was that Maureen *wasn't* open; she just pretended to be. What she *really* was was a sneak. And I know, because I saw her kiss Tim Banister behind the arbor when we were all at Green Park. She kissed him, holding him close and looking as if she was going to swallow him whole. Then she smiled radiantly at him and ran one of her long pink fingernails slowly down his cheek, leaving a mark. Later she led everyone to laugh at him, because he had this bloody line like a dueling scar by his mouth. "Lost a battle with a bush" is what she said.

And once I overheard her call Marybeth Meacham something awful—much worse than any 'tupid—over and over until Marybeth cried and promised to let Maureen copy off her next chemistry test.

Perhaps you could say I was being a sneak, too, overseeing and overhearing all that stuff and more; only I did it because I wanted Thom to know.

But whenever I told him, he only sighed and said, "She's so beautiful, Little Why." As if that excused everything.

As if that excused *anything*.

The night of the prom was their one-year anniversary. Thom had started dating Maureen at the last prom. Or at least he had stolen her from Giles Martin, the graduating football captain. Or had been given her by Giles. It was never exactly clear in my mind.

Thom didn't look happy all that day.

"Why are you unhappy?" I asked. I was always oversensitive to his moods.

He didn't answer. Just continued getting dressed in the rented midnight blue tux. He was to be crowned king of the prom, so he had to look really snazzy. Maureen, of course, was the queen. I tied his tie for him. Mom had wanted to but had made the usual hash of it.

"Why so glum?" I tried again as I pulled the ends through.

He gave me a little smile that left a deep dimple in his right cheek. "Mind your own beeswax," he said—a phrase he'd once heard in an old movie and we both used to mean "bug off."

"Why?" I was nothing if not persistent.

He kissed me on the forehead, picked up the box with Maureen's corsage in it, and left. I could hear the smooth rumble of the Firebird as he eased it out of the driveway.

And I never saw him again.

Except once.

The night of my sophomore prom I had the flu and couldn't go. I think I was just as happy about missing it as I would have been if I'd gone.

The night of my junior prom my appendix erupted before my date even arrived, and I ended up in the hospital in my lavender voile dress. Again, I wasn't particularly unhappy about not going.

But I was senior class president and *had* to make an appearance at the senior prom. I was prepared for disaster, of course, but actually got all the way to the dance with Johnny Sample, whose height was the only thing that recommended him. That and the fact that he had a car.

We hobbled around the floor a couple of times—and called it dancing—before I excused myself and went to the girls' bathroom. I managed to outlast the other girls who were primping and preening. They all disappeared together, back to their dates, when the band started up a bunny hop. Johnny Sample was not worth the hurry.

Sighing, I leaned against the sink counter and thought about Thom and his senior prom. And about Maureen. " 'Tupid!" I said aloud.

And suddenly there she was, a kind of hazy but still beautiful outline, blowing smoke rings and laughing that tinkly laugh. She was in the off-the-shoulder, belle-of-the-ball dress that she'd had on five years earlier. It should have looked silly and dated but didn't.

Maureen.

"Why?" I asked, getting right to the point.

She turned, as if noticing me for the first time, and threw the cigarette into the sink. It sizzled there for a moment, then disappeared.

"Do you *really* want to know?" she asked. Her voice held a challenge.

"Don't be . . . 'tupid!" I said. "Of course I want to know."

"Knowledge isn't all it's cracked up to be," she said. "And if you hadn't made it to the prom . . ." She stopped and held out her hazy hand.

I reached for it, expecting to touch nothing more than air. But I found my wrist being gripped by her strong fingers, and they were cold and hot at the same time, like being touched by dry ice.

"Hey!" I said loudly, startled.

She laughed, the same sly, tinkly laugh she had when we'd played cards that first time. I hadn't liked the sound of it then. Trust me, it was worse now.

The bathroom walls began to shimmer and then drift apart, like the curtains of a stage set. And there in front of us was Thom's Firebird, not rusted and dripping, as I had seen it on the TV reports, but shining and new, lovingly polished.

In the front seat was a dark, shadowy driver.

Thom.

Suddenly, after years of wishing for it, I did not want to see him.

"Get in," Maureen said, pulling me with her, her icy fingers uncompromising.

"I'm not sure..." I said.

"We're way past not sure," she said, opening the passenger door, sliding over real close to the driver, and pulling me with her. The door shut by itself.

"Thom," I said, my voice shaking, and the shadow driver turned.

I didn't want to look, I was afraid to look, but I looked anyway.

It was Thom, and it wasn't. Somehow I could see the skull beneath the familiar curve of cheek, the death undisguised by the dimple.

"Little Why," the driver said, in a voice that was just a scratchy recollection of Thom's voice. There was real regret in those two words. I know, because I'd always been oversensitive to his moods.

"I love you, Thom," I said. "I've missed you."

He didn't answer, but Maureen laughed. How nasty that laugh was, not tinkly at all but more like a bell scratching over a slate board. It made me shiver, even more than the icy grip on my wrist.

"Drive," Maureen said to Thom.

The car slid into motion effortlessly. The tires made no sound at all.

"Where are we going?" I asked. But even then I knew. This car had only one destination; it ran on a single preordained track. It turned deftly onto the road that led to the quarry.

As we rolled along, Thom and Maureen began to argue; and the argument was as smooth as the car. They spoke their lines as if they were bad actors in a play, all rote and no emotion. After all, they must have been having the same argument for years.

"You kissed Banister, didn't you," Thom said. "Why?"

"And others," Maureen taunted.

"Why?" he asked again.

"You sound like your little sister."

"And you sound..."

"'Tupid?" In her mouth the word was charmless and ugly, but he didn't seem to notice.

For a long stretch of road they were silent. In fact the only sound was the horrid beating of my heart, thumping out what should have been the rhythm of the wheels.

At the crossroads, Thom stopped.

"Drive to the quarry," Maureen said.

"No, Thom!" My voice seemed to bounce off of their quarrel, making no impact at all.

"I'll show you what a real kiss is," Maureen said. "Then you won't worry about Banister and the others."

"No, Thom!" I cried again.

"I don't want a real kiss," Thom said. "I want..."

"What *do* you want?" Maureen asked, and her outline began to solidify. "Anything you want can be had."

"For a price," I screamed. "No, Thom."

"I want..." Thom said miserably, "I want to be free of you."

Clearly the answer was not what she expected, and just as they neared the edge of the quarry, she stamped her left foot—a little-

117

girl gesture that was as stupid and as silly as she. Only her foot hit Thom's on the gas pedal, and the car leaped forward.

I suppose Thom could have slammed his left foot on the brake. He certainly had the reflexes for it. But he didn't. He just let out a deep and deeply grateful sigh, as if Maureen had made up his mind for him.

"Thom!" I screamed as the car moved forward. Maureen's cold hand was still hard on my wrist. It was clear that she wanted to take me with them into death.

For a moment, the shadow that was my brother turned its head. He saw—and didn't see me. "I love you, Little Why," he breathed as the Firebird tipped over the edge. "Take care of Mom." Then the car began to fall down and down and down into the dark quarry.

I may have screamed then, or cried out, but I could not pull loose of Maureen's icy grip. Expecting a crash when we hit the cold waters, I braced myself, but we slid in as smoothly as a spoon into cream.

The water cocooned us in darkness and some began to seep through the doors and windows. And still the car went down and down.

"Thom!" I cried, feeling around for the overhead light. When it came on, the inside of the car was lit in a creepy, yellowish glow. Thom lay with his head against the wheel, unconscious. Maureen, her big eyes wide open, seemed to stare at nothing.

"Thom!" I called again. But I knew they were both dead long before.

"I'm sorry, Thom," I whispered. "I don't belong here." Then I did what I should have done six years before. I kicked at Maureen until I got away from her grip, taking three of her bone fingers with me. Rolling down the window enough to wriggle through, I rose through the murky waters to the surface.

I swam weakly to the opposite side of the quarry, where there were steps leading up to a ramp, and pulled myself ashore. One of my red shoes was gone.

I wondered what the police had made of the red shoe, the open window. I didn't remember either of those in the report of five years ago. I wondered what my mother would think when I came home soaking wet, around my wrist a bracelet of bone.

But I didn't care. I was remembering vividly what the ghost Maureen had said. That knowledge wasn't all it was cracked up to be.

She was wrong. And still 'tupid after all these years.

Knowledge of how Thom died had set me free. Free to get on with my life.

And Thom to get on with his death.

This is true. Every single word of it. I didn't know that I was going to write this until I sat down one rainy morning, sure I had nothing in my head at all. The poem came out in a rush, a kind of catharsis, I think, because it had been an awful week: Two friends died, two more had recurrences of cancers that had been in remission, and a friend's daughter was found to be HIV positive. Oh yes—and Princess Diana was killed that week in a car crash. I was in Britain at the time, and the news media was full of it day after day after day.

My Own Ghosts

I am often visited
by the dear dead
in the cemetery of night,
when the living sleep so well
they cannot disturb
the little graves in my mind.
My mother, book in lap,
snugs into a stuffed chair,
haloed by a curl of cigarette smoke.
My father, with his great kite,
slaps a cap on his head,
slamming out of the door.
Uncle Harry and Aunt Iz,
still locked in an argument,
turn as one to hug me.
Honey opens her arms.
And wagging a black tail,
almost indistinguishable

from the surrounding night,
Mandy grins a doggy greeting,
that same toothy smile
that frightened the mailman
and sent at least one of my
ardent boyfriends
running back to his car
without a good-night kiss.

Live long enough,
and we all have such ghosts
prospering in the dark.